Cradling Kira in one arm, Skylar stood on tiptoe and reached up and circled his neck with her hand

Cooper tensed, but it didn't stop her. She stroked his roughened skin and felt the texture of his thick hair curling into his collar.

At her touch, his eyes darkened and she pulled him toward her, meeting the firm line of his lips gently, softly. One touch and emotions exploded around them. He cupped her face and took over the kiss with a deep, yearning intensity. He tasted of sunshine and the outdoors. As he caressed her lips, a sensual heat built in her and mingled with the wildness in both of them. His callused hands held her face, but all she felt was his power—in her and all around her. A gentle power that was riveting. Evocative. Real.

The kiss went on and on, bonding them together in a new way—as a man and as a woman fully aware of the differences.

Dear Reader,

Welcome to the last book in THE BELLES OF TEXAS trilogy. This one is close to my heart, and I'll tell you why. The heroine's four-year-old daughter, Kira, has juvenile rheumatoid arthritis, a disease I'm familiar with. When I was planning this book, I knew Skylar's child had something wrong with her, but I didn't know what. One day I went for a checkup, and the nurse suggested I give her juvenile arthritis. I should probably tell you I was diagnosed with rheumatoid arthritis when I was eighteen.

I hesitated. I deal with the disease daily and I didn't want to give it to a little girl, even if she was fictional. The nurse said I was well acquainted with how rheumatoid arthritis affects a person so the story should be easy to write. It wasn't. Every pain Kira Belle suffered, I felt, too. But I made sure she had loving people all around her, just like I have in my life. I was pleased with the way the story turned out, even though I cringed a lot while writing it.

Some scenes in the book were taken from my childhood and I admit I used artistic license with the well scene. Enjoy Skylar's story. I promise it will keep you on the edge of your seat.

With love and thanks,

Linda Warren

P.S. It's the highlight of my day to hear from readers. You can e-mail me at Lw1508@aol.com or write me at P.O. Box 5182, Bryan, TX 77805 or visit my Web site at www.lindawarren.net. Your letters will be answered.

Skylar's Outlaw
Linda Warren

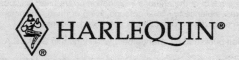

TORONTO • NEW YORK • LONDON
AMSTERDAM • PARIS • SYDNEY • HAMBURG
STOCKHOLM • ATHENS • TOKYO • MILAN • MADRID
PRAGUE • WARSAW • BUDAPEST • AUCKLAND

PLEASE RECYCLE · THIS PRODUCT IS RECYCLABLE

Recycling programs
for this product may
not exist in your area.

ISBN-13: 978-0-373-71610-4

SKYLAR'S OUTLAW

www.eHarlequin.com

Printed in U.S.A.

ABOUT THE AUTHOR

Award-winning, bestselling author Linda Warren has written twenty-three books for the Harlequin Superromance and Harlequin American Romance lines. She grew up in the farming and ranching community of Smetana, Texas, the only girl in a family of boys. She loves to write about Texas, and from time to time scenes and characters from her childhood show up in her books. Linda lives in College Station, Texas, not far from her birthplace, with her husband, Billy, and a menagerie of wild animals, from Canada geese to bobcats. Visit her Web site at www.lindawarren.net.

Books by Linda Warren

HARLEQUIN SUPERROMANCE

1167—A BABY BY CHRISTMAS
1121—THE RIGHT WOMAN
1250—FORGOTTEN SON
1314—ALL ROADS LEAD
    TO TEXAS
1354—SON OF TEXAS
1375—THE BAD SON
1440—ADOPTED SON
1470—TEXAS BLUFF
1499—ALWAYS A MOTHER
1574—CAITLYN'S PRIZE*
1592—MADISON'S CHILDREN*

HARLEQUIN AMERICAN ROMANCE

1042—THE CHRISTMAS
    CRADLE
1089—CHRISTMAS,
    TEXAS STYLE
    "Merry Texmas"
1102—THE COWBOY'S
    RETURN
1151—ONCE A COWBOY
1226—TEXAS HEIR
1249—THE SHERIFF OF
    HORSESHOE, TEXAS

*The Belles of Texas

I dedicate this book to the millions of people
who suffer with arthritis.

May they soon find a cure.

ACKNOWLEDGMENTS

A special thanks to:

J.O. Siegert for answering my many questions
about water wells and ranching.

Mark Fuller, DVM, for always coming
to the rescue for all my animal problems.

Micki Gutierrez, RN, for offering a great suggestion.

And, Lara Chapman for kindly sharing
information on Giddings, Texas.

All errors are strictly mine.

CHAPTER ONE

SKYLAR BELLE HATED BEING ignored, especially by a man.

Especially by him.

The padded chair squeaked against the hardwood floor as she moved uneasily due to her infuriated thoughts. But she wasn't going to put up with his blatant rudeness one more day.

"The ex-con has to go." She said the words loudly and clearly, with an angry undertone, determined to snare her sister's attention. What she got was silence.

Damn freakin' silence.

Her oldest sister, Caitlyn, sat transfixed with her hand on her stomach, a goofy expression Sky had never seen before plastered on her face. The look seemed out of place on her responsible, bossy sister. Finding out you're pregnant could do that to a woman, though. Skylar knew that.

Her other sister, Madison, held her four-month-old daughter on her shoulder, burping her and occasionally kissing the baby's cheek. Maddie was enraptured and totally oblivious to everyone else in the room.

Neither sister had heard a word she'd said.

She might need a cannon or a bomb to break into their thoughts.

"She's asleep," Maddie whispered, gingerly getting

to her feet. "I'll put her down and then we can talk. I know you said something, Sky."

"Yes, and I'd appreciate it if you two could focus." They were in the study, having their monthly meeting to discuss the High Five ranch. Or trying to have the meeting, was more accurate.

As Maddie left, Cait rubbed her flat belly. "I can hardly believe a little person is growing in here."

Sky leaned back, studying her sister with the black hair and Belle blue eyes. The ranch had always been Cait's top priority, but now Sky couldn't even get her attention to discuss it. "I never thought you'd be this sappy."

Cait looked up, her eyes as bright as the May sun peeping through the study windows. "Judd and I are so happy."

"And I'm happy for you, but could we please talk about High Five?"

"Of course, but we have to wait for Maddie. She's busy with the baby." Cait crossed her legs, that goofy expression still intact. "We thought Maddie would never have children, and now she has three. That's so wonderful. No one deserves it more than our sister."

"Yes." Sky picked up a crystal paperweight and the scent of vanilla drifted to her from the candle sitting beside it—one of Maddie's touches to the study.

Her sweet, loving sister had been diagnosed with ovarian cancer when she was twenty-eight, and was unable to have children. But then she'd met Walker, a man with three kids who needed a woman in his life. They fell deeply in love. Maddie deserved her happily-ever-after, but Sky knew that type of relationship wasn't for her.

Cait was the responsible one, Maddie the sweet one

and Sky was known as the wild one. Their three different mothers had all been married at one time to Dane Belle. Sky's mother had married five times, so Sky never had a stable environment, except when she visited her father, grandmother and sisters on the High Five ranch in Texas. Now her dad was gone and the ranch he loved had been left to his daughters. Their goal was to keep it going.

Since Cait's mother had died in childbirth, she'd been raised on the ranch. Sky had thought her sister would never leave the place of her birth. Then a neighboring rancher, Judd Calhoun, had wooed her away. Now the responsibility for High Five was on Sky's shoulders, and she didn't take that lightly. She had to make her sisters understand her point of view.

Clearing her throat, she said, "We're all dealing with motherhood, but we still have to run this ranch."

Cait lifted an eyebrow. "Is bitchy getting responsible?"

Sky groaned at the nickname, but she had to admit she could be a bitch if the occasion arose.

"I've always been responsible." She tried to keep a straight face.

"Yeah…"

Maddie slipped back into the room. "Sorry that took so long, but Georgie had the baby's blanket tied around his neck, preparing to jump off the back of the sofa as Spider-Man. Kira was right behind him."

Sky was immediately on her feet. Her child was her life. "Is she—"

"She's fine." Maddie motioned for her to sit down. "I had a talk with Georgie, and he won't do it again."

"Your talks are not exactly stern. I'd better—"

"Georgie won't disobey," Maddie said on a firm note. "Gran and Etta are watching them. So what do you want to talk about?"

This was it. She had their attention.

"Oh, darn." Maddie glanced sideways at her shoulder. "I have milk all over me."

Sky felt like bumping her head against the desk in frustration. Instead, she opened a drawer and threw her a box of tissues. "You smell great, too."

Maddie made a face and caught the box. "Sour milk is my perfume these days. Walker loves it, so we're both happy."

Losing patience, Sky clapped her hands. "Listen up. We need to talk about High Five."

"I've been here thirty minutes and nothing's been said."

"Because you're not listening," Sky shouted at Cait. "You're in la-la land."

Both sisters stared at her, and she leaped right in with what she had to say. "After the destruction of the hurricane and the fire, High Five is finally making a turn for the better. I think that's what Dad wanted for us—to realize the importance of our heritage and to work together to secure it. That's why he put that ridiculous clause in his will that the ranch had to be sold to Judd if it wasn't showing a profit in six months."

"Dad knew I'd fight that like a hellcat and call y'all home to help, especially since I'd jilted Judd fourteen years before and considered him my archenemy." Cait's voice softened. "He also knew that if he pitted Judd and me against each other, we'd fall in love all over again."

"He had a plan and it worked," Maddie said, wiping at her blouse. "Even though he'd left the ranch in dire straits because of his gambling debts, he knew we'd pull together to save High Five. He wanted us to feel the same pride he had in home and family."

Cait's eyes grew wistful. "It's ironic that Dad, who was the king of spoiling and pampering and who repeatedly told us we needed husbands to take care of us, took the biggest gamble of his life when he bet those same daughters would rescue High Five."

There was silence for a moment as they each thought about their father. Sky knew they were getting sidetracked, and she had to bring the discussion back to her problem.

"As I said, the ranch is finally showing a profit and I want to keep it that way." She gripped the paperweight. "I can't do that with Cooper Yates as foreman. He has to go. I've put up with his insolent attitude long enough."

Maddie's head shot up. "I don't understand why you can't get along with Cooper."

"Why do I have to? I own this ranch."

"You're a part owner," Cait reminded her.

She gritted her teeth. "When Maddie got married, I agreed to take over running the place, but I can't do that with someone who ignores me and my orders."

Maddie and Cait shared a glance, and it irritated Sky when they did that. She was always the odd one out.

Cait got to her feet. "Bottom line, Sky, this ranch won't survive without Cooper's expertise. He puts in fourteen- to sixteen-hour days without any overtime pay. He's dedicated to High Five, so I suggest you learn to get along, because Cooper stays."

Sky rose to her feet, ready for battle. "You don't get to make that decision alone."

"I vote with Cait." Maddie placed the tissues on the desk. "Cooper stays."

Sky tucked her naturally curly red hair behind her ears. "I have a child and I thought you'd be more considerate of Kira. I don't want her around an ex-con."

"You know Cooper was framed for killing those horses, and all the charges were dropped." Cait reached for her purse on the floor. "What else is bothering you?"

Sky had to be honest. "Not all the charges were dropped. He almost beat to death the man who framed him, and he's still on probation for the assault. I don't want a man with that kind of temper around my daughter."

Maddie picked up her diaper bag. "I'd trust Coop with my kids any day of the week. I've worked with him and I know he's a good man who's had some bad breaks. Just cut him some slack."

"I can't believe you two." Sky flung up her hands. "I ask for your help and you're telling me to deal with him."

"That's it." Cait glanced at her watch. "I've got to run. Judd has a decorator coming to give ideas on a nursery." She slung her purse strap over her shoulder. "As if I need ideas, but I'll cooperate because I'm such a good wife."

Sky's patience snapped. "If High Five needs Cooper Yates so badly, then I might as well not be here. I'll pack my things and leave." She glared at her older sister. "That's my bottom line."

"That's just like you, Sky," Cait shot back, just as Sky knew she would. Their relationship had always been volatile because they were so alike in their fiery temperament. "It's your way or nothing."

"It's not about having my way. I can't work with the man."

"All right," Cait shouted. "I'll take over running High Five."

"Cait!" Maddie was quick to come to her defense. "You can't do that. You're going to have a baby."

"With Sky being so stubborn, I don't see any other way. I'll have to come back."

Sky felt like a fifth grader, being mean for no reason. Except she *had* a reason.

"Cait…" Maddie trailed off as Gran walked into the room. Their grandmother's hair was beautifully white and curled into a knot at her nape. In slacks, a multicolored blouse and sensible shoes, Dorthea Belle looked much younger than her seventy-seven years. Sky had often thought she had an ageless beauty, with a softness and a fragility that was very striking. Even in slacks Gran wore her pearls.

Southern manners had been instilled into her, and she tried her best to impress those views on her granddaughters. Somehow her teachings had missed the mark, but all three sisters were aware of Gran's position on life, women and their roles. They respected her enough never to hurt her.

"What's this I hear about leaving and coming back?"

Maddie hoisted the diaper bag higher on her shoulder and walked forward. Linking her arm through Gran's, she asked, "Have you been listening at the door?"

"Certainly not." Gran stiffened her shoulders. "A lady would never do such a thing."

"Then how did you hear?" Maddie continued in her pleasant, soothing way.

"Cait and Sky were shouting, my baby. That's how I heard." Gran looked at Cait. "What's this nonsense about you coming back to High Five?"

Cait stared at Sky, who wasn't sure how to explain this to Gran. *Damn Cooper Yates.*

Gran patted Maddie's hand. "Since your sisters seem to be tongue-tied, tell me what's going on."

As if it was the easiest thing in the world, Maddie started to explain. "Sky has a problem working with Cooper."

"What? That's ridiculous. Cooper is a very nice and polite young man."

"We were trying to explain that to Sky, but she feels differently, and we have to respect her feelings. That's the reason Cait offered to come back."

"Respect, my ass," Cait whispered under her breath.

"Cait's not coming back to High Five to work," Gran stated firmly. "She has a husband, a home, a baby on the way, and she doesn't belong here, running a ranch." Gran patted Maddie's hand again. "Neither do you, so go home to your husbands. Sky and I will sort this out. If worst comes to worst, I can run the ranch."

A collective gasp echoed around the room. Cait mouthed at Sky, *I'm going to kill you.*

"I can see you, Caitlyn," Gran stated.

"Gran…"

She held up a hand. "Go home, my baby. That's where you belong."

"But you *can't* run this ranch." Cait couldn't leave well enough alone.

Their grandmother bristled. "You don't *think* I can."

"Cait didn't mean that." As usual, peacemaker Maddie tried to soothe the ruffled feathers.

"Good." Gran nodded. "Sky and I will talk about this. We'll let you know how it turns out. Goodbye, my babies."

"I'm going to kill you," Cait muttered once again as

she walked out the door. Maddie looked anxious, but followed her.

Don't go. Don't go.

As upset as she was with her sisters, Sky did not want to face her grandmother alone. Gran would pick away at her emotions like a buzzard gnaws at a carcass, laying bare every fear, every anxiety she kept hidden.

Gran took Maddie's seat, her back straight, her hands folded in her lap. "Now, young lady, what's the problem?"

Oh, God. When Gran sat as a proper Southern woman and called her "young lady," Sky knew she was in trouble. However, she wasn't a little girl or a teenager anymore. She was now an adult and able to handle her grandmother.

Yeah, a little voice mocked her, *like when cows can vote.*

She pushed the nervousness away and decided to be honest. "Gran…"

"Just so we're clear." Gran held up the forefinger on her left hand, and Sky noticed her platinum-and-diamond wedding rings. Sky had always loved them. When Cait married, Sky had felt sure Gran would give them to her, but Judd had had his own ideas for Cait's rings, as Walker had for Maddie's. Sky was the only granddaughter left, and she would never wed. She would never again open her heart to a scum like Todd Spencer, who had shredded her emotions like confetti.

"You are not leaving High Five." Gran's declaration broke through her musings. "Kira loves it here and you can't keep uprooting her. She needs stability. It's time to stand up to Todd's parents, but that's another discussion. Right now I want to talk about Cooper."

For once Sky would rather talk about Cooper, too. Ever since Todd's parents had found out about Kira, they'd wanted a paternity test done, in hopes of gaining custody of their only grandchild. Sky had been on the run since then. She would fight with her last breath before she'd let the wealthy Spencers take her child.

She forced Todd's parents out of her mind. "Cooper doesn't like me and I'm not that crazy about him, either. I don't see how we can continue to work together."

"How do you know he doesn't like you?"

"He won't speak to me and he avoids me. When I tell him to do something, he ignores me."

"Well, that's just rude."

Sky blinked. Hot damn. Gran was on her side. She didn't expect this.

"But, my baby, you've been rude to him, too. Cooper doesn't even eat at the house anymore because of you and your intolerance. I've taught you better than that. Being part owner of this ranch gives you certain rights, but prejudice isn't one of them."

"Gran!" She could feel Gran stripping away all her defenses and her rights as she envisioned them, exposing a painful reality that wedged its way into her heart— she'd disappointed her grandmother once again.

Gran shouldn't be able to ignite her guilt. But she managed to, because Sky loved her. Gran and Sky's father had been the only stability she'd ever known in her life. And disappointing them had always taken a slice of her pride. Like now.

"But my granddaughter will not be treated that way. I will have a word with Cooper." Gran slowly pushed to her feet.

Guilt screamed full blast through her conscience, awakening a barefaced truth. Since when had she needed anyone to fight her battles? This wasn't Cait's, Maddie's or Gran's problem. *It was hers.* And it was time to stop acting like a fifth grader and run this ranch with authority, as Cait and Maddie had. Cooper Yates would not make her turn tail and run.

"No, Gran." Sky rose to her feet with confidence, stopping her at the door. "I'll talk with Cooper. It's my job and this time he will not ignore me."

Gran fingered her pearls. "I wondered what had happened to your fighting spirit."

She winced. "Momentary insanity."

"Baby, give the man a chance. High Five can't afford to lose him."

"Cait said the same thing."

"Well, then, enough said. Pull up your big-girl panties and get this done…the Belle way."

Sky's laughter echoed around the room. "Gran, you've said that since I was small, and I still don't know what the hell it means."

"But you get the gist? And no cursing, please."

Sky wrapped an arm around the old woman's thin shoulders. "Yes, ma'am."

"That's all that matters, and thank you. I really didn't want to saddle up in the morning."

Sky stopped and stared at her grandmother. "You had no intention of saddling up. You played me like a fine-tuned violin. You knew if you made me see how selfish I was being, I'd relent."

Gran shrugged. "Whatever works."

"Mommy. Mommy," Kira called, running from the parlor, with Etta, the housekeeper, on her heels.

Before the child reached Sky, she fell headlong onto the hardwood floor. Loud cries filled the room. Sky immediately scooped her up.

Don't ask if she's hurt. Don't ask.

Her four-year-old daughter had been diagnosed with juvenile rheumatoid arthritis, and the doctor warned about constantly asking if Kira was hurting. It would make the child paranoid and deeply aware of her condition. Kira would tell her if she was in pain. Still, Sky couldn't help thinking about it constantly.

Kira's cries grew louder. Sky rubbed her back. "You're okay, precious. Shh. Mommy's here."

Raising her head from Sky's shoulder, she wiped at her eyes. "I fall down."

Sky kissed a wet cheek. "Yes, you did." Kira fell a lot but the doctor said that was normal. There was nothing normal about her baby hurting, though.

Kira's right knee was red and swollen this morning. Her child living in pain kept her on tenterhooks, and she tried not to let it show. She didn't always accomplish that.

"How about a nap?"

Kira stopped rubbing her eyes. "'Kay. Is Georgie coming back?"

"Not today, precious."

"I wanna play with Georgie."

"Maybe tomorrow."

"And we'll have some chocolate pudding when you wake up." Gran kissed Kira. "I love you."

"Love you, too." Kira rested her head against Sky's shoulder again and all her motherly instincts kicked in, feelings she thought she would never have. But the moment she'd first held her baby, her whole personality seemed to change. Kira depended on her, needed her. Sky had never had full responsibility for another person and at first it had overwhelmed her. Now it was natural.

She stroked her daughter's red curly hair, hair just like her own, as were her blue eyes. Very little of Todd was evident in Kira, and Sky was grateful for that.

Slowly, she made her way up the stairs to their bedroom. Kira really needed her own room, but Sky was afraid she wouldn't hear her if she needed her during the night. Besides, it was just the two of them, and probably always would be.

After she gave Kira some children's liquid Tylenol and settled her down for a nap, Sky planned to have an up-close-and-personal meeting with Mr. Cooper Yates.

And this time he wasn't ignoring her.

WITH A KNOT in his gut, Cooper watched Cait and Maddie drive away. He strode into the barn, his jaw clenched. The redhead had called a family meeting and he knew exactly what it was about. She wanted to get rid of him.

If he knew Cait and Maddie—and he did, since he'd worked side by side with both—he couldn't see them going along with such a plan. But they were sisters, and owners of High Five. He was just the hired hand. A cowboy.

He threw a saddle over his brown-and-white paint, Rebel, and tightened the cinch. The horse did a quick side step and reared his head. Cooper had just bought and broken the gelding, which was still fidgety. But he'd settle down.

The calluses on Cooper's hands rubbed against the leather strap. He was a working man—work kept his demons at bay. Cait had understood that. So had Maddie. But the redhead wanted him gone, and he wondered if she'd get her wish. It didn't matter to him. He didn't know if he could continue to work for the woman, anyway. Maybe it was time for him to move on.

To what?

Dane Belle had given him a job when no one else would. High Five was his home now and the redhead wasn't getting rid of him. Besides, he was on probation and couldn't leave the county. He was here to stay. Once he made that decision the knot in his stomach eased.

But not for long.

The redhead was coming his way.

CHAPTER TWO

"MAY I SPEAK WITH YOU, please?" Sky was determined to be polite, using her best manners, as Gran would want her to.

"It's a free country." The deep drawl came from the other side of the horse, and the man made no move to look at her or to acknowledge her presence.

She gritted her teeth, but his insolence wasn't going to cause her to lose her temper. "We have to work together so could you please look at me?"

He lowered the stirrup, raised his head and glared at her over the top of the saddle. For the first time, she noticed his eyes were a deep green, not brown as she'd thought. Green and cold as a frozen pond. She actually felt a chill and wrapped her arms around her waist.

"I'm guessing you want to talk because the meeting with Cait and Maddie didn't go your way." His voice was as cold as his eyes. Even so, it had a gravelly intone that would be attractive if it hadn't been delivered with such an edge.

She bit her lip as fiery retorts zinged through her head. The cow dogs lay at his feet, but they were looking at her almost as if they were waiting for her next words.

She took a step closer, surprising herself at her calmness. "No. It didn't go my way. I find it very hard to work with you when it's crystal clear you don't like me."

His jaw tightened, as did the chiseled lines of his lean face. "Like you're crazy about having an ex-con on the property."

"Okay. I'll admit I have a problem with that." She tugged her fingers through her frizzy red curls. God, it was a humid day, and her hair was a mess. Not that the man on the other side of the horse noticed. And nor did she want him to. *Focus.* "But Cait, Maddie and Gran are on your side, so let's make this work."

The dogs rose to their feet, and she knew that was a signal the man was about to mount his horse. She grabbed the reins so the animal couldn't move. The horse moved nervously and tried to rear its head, but she held tight. Her heart ricocheted off her ribs from the anger blazing in his eyes.

But she didn't back down, though it was hard not to. The man stood at least six foot two, with a whipcord body and broad shoulders. Faded jeans and a pearl-snap shirt molded his muscled frame. He pulled his worn and dusty Stetson low so it hid most of his brooding expression.

She had a split second to get her words out before he exploded. "We have to run this ranch together, and you might as well accept that. If you have something against me, just say so and we'll talk it out. But High Five comes first and we have to put our differences aside. I'd appreciate your cooperation. And Gran would like it if you'd have your meals at the house as you did before."

His eyes seared hers like a hot iron as he jerked the reins from her hand. Without a word he swung into the saddle, spurred the paint and shot out of the barn like a rocket, the dogs following.

At his high-handedness, she freed the padlock she'd had on her emotions and kicked at the dirt. "You low-down, sorry bastard! You son of a bitch!"

"Girl, where did you learn words like that?" Rufus, Etta's husband, came through from the corral, leading his horse.

She gulped a long breath. "Sorry, Rufus. I was letting off steam."

Rufus was in his seventies, tall, lean and slightly bow-legged. He'd spent every day since he was a kid in the saddle, except for the years he'd been in prison.

"Cut the boy some slack."

"I was just trying to do that, but he ignored me once again." She frowned. "Why does he dislike me?"

Ru tipped back his hat. "Now, girl, that's a mighty powerful question."

The old tomcat that lived in the barn darted out and scurried across bales of hay stacked in a corner. The sweet, pungent scent of alfalfa reached her nostrils. That smell always reminded her of home, of High Five.

"Could be he took his cue from you?"

She brought her gaze back to Rufus. "What?"

"You never hid how you felt about him."

"Oh." What was it with the elders on this ranch? They were on a spear-Skylar campaign, making her aware of every lousy fault she had.

Ru patted his mare, Dixie. "You never felt that way about me, did you?"

Her eyes flew to his clouded ones. "Of course not. I've known you all my life and you're part of our family."

"I killed a man, though."

"You were trying to keep him from murdering his girlfriend. You never meant to hurt him."

"But I drank a lot back then. Etta didn't like it. I went to bars, too. Etta didn't like that, either, but I kept going. Maybe I wouldn't have been so quick to hit the guy if I'd been sober. One swing from my fist and he was dead." Ru flexed his right hand. "Sometimes in life those bad breaks happen. Prison woke me up, and I've always been grateful for the people who stood by me, like Mr. Bart, Miss Dorie, Dane and my Etta. Couldn't have gotten through it without them."

A lump formed in Sky's throat. Ru was a quiet man. He rarely spoke and he never talked about that time in his life.

"Coop's had no one," he continued. "His mother died and his dad beat him regularly as a kid. Finally, he ran away and made it on his own. He was doing good. A lot of ranchers wanted to hire him, and then that man framed him to get the insurance money from the thoroughbred horses. In anger, Coop lashed out. I don't blame him. I probably would have done the same thing, but it changed his life forever. No one trusts him. It's like a brand he wears every day—'ex-con.'"

She swallowed the lump, feeling lower than dirt. And Ru wasn't through.

"Have you ever seen a ranch this size run by two men, one of them getting on in years? Coop's a work-horse. We have corn, maize, coastal and alfalfa planted. It will all have to be harvested at about the same time. Coop will get very little sleep during those weeks. This is his home now. He has no family but the one he's made here at High Five."

Ru placed a worn boot into the stirrup and mounted his horse. The leather creaked from his weight. Dixie pranced around, ready to go. "If you love High Five, you'll adjust your attitude. Remember, Dane Belle is watching." After delivering that startling news, he slowly rode out of the barn.

Sky sank onto a bale of hay and let the sounds and smells of the old barn take her away. Most people would think the scents of manure, horses, dogs and hay unpleasant. Nevertheless, it brought back her childhood— days of fun and laughter and of being loved. She had very little of that in her mother's world. They moved so much her suitcase was always packed.

Julia was good at spouting the same old line: "I'm gonna find the right man this time, sugar." But the right man for her mother never appeared. She kept looking, though. Julia was a beautiful redhead who could attract any man's attention, but she could never hold it.

The last one, Everett Coleman, had just about done them both in. Sky never liked him, but her mother was crazy about the arrogant, egotistical Texan. Mostly, Julia was crazy about money, and the way Everett lavished it on her. The only thing Sky liked about the man was that he lived in Texas and she could visit her father when she visited her mother.

It amazed her that Julia had stayed married to the man for five years. When he started having financial problems, her mother was out the door. That was four years ago. Sky never asked what had happened. Her mother's marriages weren't her favorite topic.

After that, she and her mother did grow closer. Julia had been a nurse before she'd married Dane Belle, and she was there when Sky needed her the most—to answer her many questions about Kira's health.

Now her mother was out to capture husband number six. Sky had vowed never to be like that, so she and Todd had moved in together for a trial period. The stupidest decision she'd ever made. She was determined to avoid repeating her mother's mistakes. In doing so, she'd fallen into the same pattern.

From the start Todd had said he never wanted kids, so they were very careful. But partying all night sometimes left "careful" at the door. When Sky told Todd she was pregnant, he'd thrown a fit, packed his things, told her she was on her own and left. She'd kept waiting for him to come back. He didn't.

As her pregnancy started to show, rumors began to emerge. A friend told her that Todd's parents knew she was pregnant and were just waiting for the baby to be born so a paternity test could be done. If the baby was Todd's, they planned to file for custody.

She dismissed the first rumor, but then a friend of Todd's told her the same thing, and she knew it was true. The Spencers were wealthy and they could take her baby with a high-priced attorney, something she couldn't afford. Her party-girl status was well-known. She wouldn't be portrayed as mother of the year.

The last four years she'd been on the run, making sure the Spencers never found her. It wasn't easy, but she had to keep Kira a secret from everyone, even her family at High Five.

As her father had said, all chicks come home to roost. She'd arrived at High Five at Christmas and decided to stay. Mainly because Maddie was getting married, and Sky was needed on the ranch. Besides, she was tired of living out of a suitcase. And Gran was right—Kira needed stability. She needed a home. That's what Sky wanted for her child.

So here she was, back at High Five, and her father's

presence was all around her, from the land he'd loved, to his collection of fine wines in the parlor, to the cigars he kept hidden in the study. Home. Family. Dad.

He'd been furious when he found out about Kira, and disappointed in Sky and her choices. That hurt. However, he'd supported her decision to keep Kira away from the Spencers, and made sure she had the money to do it.

"Spitfire, someday you're going to have to grow up and face this." God, she thought of his words often.

The tomcat eased around her on the bale of hay. "Hey there, Tom. Are you going to keep me company? Everyone else is on my backside, and I might just have to admit they have a reason. It's hell when that happens."

The cat curled into a comfy position and Sky rose to her feet. What was she going to do about Cooper Yates? All the way to the house the question plagued her.

She'd never had a problem with men before. Not that it was something she was proud of, but getting them to fall over themselves for her came relatively easy. It was a talent she'd inherited from her mother. Why hadn't Cooper been bowled over by her?

Motherhood. Since she'd become a mother, her life and views had changed drastically. Protecting Kira, keeping her safe and happy, was Sky's top priority. She saw Cooper as a threat to Kira's safety, and had acted accordingly.

Or was it more? Something about the way he'd looked at her when she'd first met him got to her. It was an I-don't-like-you stare. She didn't understand it, and at the time, she'd felt it was his problem, not hers. Now she wasn't so sure.

CYBIL SPENCER WAITED impatiently as her husband talked on the phone.

"Well?" she demanded when he clicked off.

"Leo Garvey, the P.I., located the apartment Skylar Belle was renting in Tennessee."

"Was she there?"

"No. She got wind he was asking questions and disappeared again."

"We pay him a lot of money. Surely he can do a better job than this. It's amateurish, and I'm tired of all this waiting." She swept back her blond bob in irritation.

Jonathan poured a shot of bourbon and raised the glass toward her. "He managed to get in the apartment before it was cleaned."

"And?"

"He found a child's hairbrush with red hair on it behind a sofa cushion." He took a swallow of the bourbon. "He's sending it to a lab for DNA testing. Now he has to get a sample of Todd's DNA, and then we'll know if the child is a Spencer."

"Pour me a gin and tonic. It's time to celebrate. After all this time, that Belle bitch is going to get what's coming to her."

WHEN COOPER RODE INTO THE barn, it was late. Darkness had settled in and the dim lightbulbs hanging from the rafters did little to chase it away.

The dogs trotted behind him, breathing heavily. Ru had quit for the day long ago. After checking the herd, Coop had sat in the grass near Crooked Creek. This time of the year, the grass was green and thriving. The cows were knee-deep in it. The hayfields were also flourishing. After the fire, he'd worried about that, but now High Five was back on track.

It was good to know that Albert Harland, the man who had set the fires to the land and house, and had attempted to kill Cait, was now serving twenty years for the crimes. That didn't erase the damages, though. Coop had to keep working so the ranch could overcome its losses.

For what?

To work with that woman?

Dismounting, he undid the saddle cinch, and with one hand swung the saddle over a sawhorse. The dogs lay down to rest. After leading the paint into the corral, Coop removed the bridle and slapped the horse's rump. The animal cantered toward the feed trough.

As Coop reentered the barn, Ru came in from the other door with a covered plate in his hand.

"You just getting in, boy? I left you two hours ago."

"Yep. I had some things I had to check."

"Like what?" Ru held the plate high as the dogs jumped to reach it.

"Just stuff."

"Miss Dorie's a might upset you're not eating at the house."

Coop hooked the bridle on a nail. "So I heard."

"C'mon, boy. Give Sky a chance."

He took the plate. "I don't give women like her chances."

"What the hell does that mean?"

"Nothing. Thanks for the food." He strolled away before Ru could grill him. The dogs followed, yapping all the way to the bunkhouse. Coop put the food on the counter, knowing he had to feed the dogs first. After being out most of the day, they were hungry.

He flipped on the front porch light and filled their bowls with a special mix of dog food he bought in Giddings. They gobbled it up, their short tails wagging. Australian blue-heelers, Boots, Bo and Booger were about the best friends he had besides Ru. They trusted him. They didn't judge him.

Removing his hat, he walked into the house and placed it on a hook. Stretching his tired muscles, he felt the aches and pains of cowboying. At thirty-five he should have his own ranch, but that bastard had taken everything from him. Now he had a record, and it followed him everywhere he went like his shadow. It was a part of him.

Being angry didn't help a thing. Coop knew that better than anyone. But when he was reminded of his past in surround sound and Technicolor, it was hard to remember.

Why did she have to come home?

With a sigh he headed to the kitchen sink, washed his hands, grabbed a fork out of a drawer and carried the plate to the table. He kept his mind blank. After years of practice, he had perfected that trait.

Tender roast, potatoes, green beans and homemade rolls—the mouthwatering aroma made his taste buds come alive. He was hungry. As he dug in, he knew he couldn't keep making extra work for Etta. He had to bite the bullet and eat at the house as he'd done before.

As much as he wanted her to, Skylar Belle wasn't going away. Chewing a mouthful of roast, he wondered what the odds were of them ever meeting again. When she'd come home for Dane's funeral, he couldn't believe his eyes. However, there was no mistaking the striking redhead with the sultry blue eyes. She'd treated him just as she had the last time he'd seen her—as if he didn't exist. She'd had no clue who he was, or if she did, she hid it well. Luckily, she hadn't stayed long and he didn't have to deal with her.

Finishing the food, he pushed back his chair, which

scraped across the old wood floor. He carried the empty plate to the sink and washed it. Etta didn't believe in paper plates. He was drying the dish when the redhead's words came back to him.

High Five comes first and we have to put our differences aside. I'd appreciate your cooperation.

Like hell...

He'd promised Cait he would do everything he could to keep High Five running smoothly, though Skylar Belle made that promise difficult. But he owed Cait, and he wouldn't go back on his word.

No matter how much personal angst it cost him.

KIRA HAD TOYS STREWN all over the parlor floor. Sky sat cross-legged, watching her child dress and undress her Barbie doll, her favorite activity. Kira loved clothes. Maybe she'd even have a career in fashion...if she had a career. There was always that fear in Sky that Kira wouldn't have much of a life, just a lot of pain and endless days of dealing with it.

The doctor had said there were three types of juvenile rheumatoid arthritis, polyarticular, pauciarticular and systemic. After much testing, and because Kira only had redness and swelling in her knees and occasionally her elbow, the doctor concluded she fell into the pauciarticular category. That was good news. With less than four joints involved, Kira could outgrow the disease or go into remission as she aged. But there was also a possibility the disease could become progressively worse. No matter what, Sky would be with her all the way.

"Time for bed, precious."

Kira shook her head. "I don't want to."

This was the hard part. Discipline. Sky held up the fingers on one hand. "Five more minutes."

Kira nodded and kept tugging a dress onto the doll.

"Cooper didn't come to supper," Gran said from the sofa. "Did you talk to him?"

Sky helped her daughter slip high heels on the doll, and realized she was biting her lip. "Yes, and I told him he was welcome."

"And…"

She looked at her grandmother. "And what?"

"What did he say?"

"Nothing, Gran. Absolutely nothing. That's his modus operandi when it comes to me."

"And Skylar Belle can't change that?"

A smile touched her lips. "Not with Southern manners."

Gran laughed, a real laugh that warmed Sky's soul. It felt good to be home with people who loved her.

"On that thought, I think it's time for all of us to go to bed." Gran rose to her feet.

Without a word Kira began to pick up her dolls and clothes. Sky found that remarkable. One word from Gran and Kira obeyed, much as she, Cait and Maddie did. Sky helped her tuck everything into a small suitcase reserved for her Barbies and then the trio headed for the stairs.

"Can I play with Georgie tomorrow?" Kira asked.

"We'll see what Aunt Maddie has to say."

Kira beamed at her. "She say yes, yes, yes."

Sky glanced at Gran. "She knows Aunt Maddie."

"Yes, she does."

They hugged on the landing. "'Night, Gran."

"'Night, my babies."

After getting Kira into bed and taking her own

shower, Sky stood looking out the window toward the bunkhouse. She could see the back of the structure and a light burning in a window on the left. That must be his bedroom.

She'd never dreamed he'd been beaten as a child. How horrific. She felt bad about how she'd treated him and how she'd thought of him like a narrow-minded simpleton.

But he had that effect on her and she couldn't explain why. It felt as if she needed to protect herself. From what? That she couldn't answer. But they definitely had a negative reaction to each other.

She crawled in beside her daughter, careful not to wake her. Dealing with Cooper, Sky had forgotten about the Spencers. But that worry was always there at the back of her mind. She prayed they'd give up their quest to find their grandchild.

Tomorrow was a new day. A day to start over. A day to forget the shadow hanging over her.

And another day to tackle Mr. Ignore Me.

Oh, he had a rude awakening coming if he thought she gave up so easily.

CHAPTER THREE

IN THE MORNING SKY carried Kira downstairs for breakfast. She placed her in a booster seat and Etta brought steaming oatmeal to the table. Fixing Kira a bowl, Sky prayed she'd eat it. Her child had very little appetite, and it was a struggle to keep her strong and healthy.

Kira played with the spoon and then glanced at her with those gorgeous blue eyes. "Can I play with Georgie today, Mommy?"

"If you eat your oatmeal and drink your milk." That was such a lame bribe, but she'd take whatever worked.

"Do Georgie eat oatmeal?"

Sky kissed her baby's cheek. "Every day. That's why he's so strong."

"I wanna be strong like Georgie." Kira shoved oatmeal into her mouth and swallowed.

Great!

"The devil's gonna get you," Etta whispered as Sky poured a cup of coffee.

"Don't tell anyone, but he already has."

The old lady grinned and Sky gave her a hug. Etta always reminded her of Granny on the old *Beverly Hillbillies* sitcom, except Etta had short permed hair.

Gran entered the kitchen already dressed for the day. Sky was still in her cotton pj's, so she kissed her and said, "Please watch Kira while I get dressed."

Gran took a seat by her great-granddaughter and Sky dashed upstairs.

In a second she had on her jeans and was stuffing the tail of a pearl-snap shirt into the waistband. She guided her braided-leather belt through the loops and buckled it. Sitting down, she slipped on her boots. *Oh, yeah. Cowgirl up.* She was ready to face Cooper Yates.

Then she turned and saw herself in the mirror. Crap! Her hair looked like a huge dust mop. She *hated* her naturally curly hair—another trait she'd inherited from her mother.

Grabbing a flat iron, her favorite tool in the whole world, she sat at the dressing table and went to work. Within minutes she had it in a manageable style, clipped back at her nape.

She took a second glance at the sprinkling of freckles across her nose. How many times had she cursed them over the years? Too many to count. Makeup would cover them, but she wasn't taking that route today. She left her fair skin clean and natural. Now she was ready.

Pausing at the door, she reached for her cell phone to call Cait.

Brenda Sue, Judd's secretary, answered. Sky groaned. The woman gave *annoying* a new meaning. "May I speak to Caitlyn, please?" She held her breath.

"Is this Sky?"

"Yes." She choked back a groan.

"I thought so. You sisters sound very alike on the phone, if you know what I mean. I might be psychic that way, too. I'm very good with voices, and some people have said—"

"Is Caitlyn there?"

"What? Oh. I'm in the office, and when they don't answer, it rings here, so I guess Judd and Cait are doing, well, you know what. Isn't it great about the baby? Judd is over the moon and Renee is not even bitchy anymore. She's finally getting a grandchild. I told Cait I'd give her some pointers, but you know Cait. She didn't take that very well. She was quite offensive, actually, and—"

"Goodbye, Brenda Sue. I'll try her cell." Sky clicked off before the woman could get in one more word, then had to take a long breath to de-stress. Finally she punched in her sister's cell number.

Cait answered almost immediately.

"I'm really surprised you haven't killed Brenda Sue by now."

Cait laughed. "Had a scintillating conversation with her?"

"More like mind-numbing."

Cait laughed again, and then said, "I hope you've come to your senses."

"Yes, and I wanted to apologize for yesterday. I can handle the ranch and Cooper."

"That's good news."

"I tend to revert to my old selfish ways every now and then, especially when I want something."

"So what changed your mind?"

"Gran. You know those talks where you think she's on your side, and it's like, oh great, she understands, but then you start to see how narrow-minded and wrong you really are?"

"Yep. I've had a few of those conversations with her myself."

"I just wanted to ease your mind about Gran and the situation. I'm really happy about the baby, and I don't understand why you won't listen to any of Brenda Sue's pointers on the topic."

Cait clicked off with an expletive that burned Sky's ears. On the way down the stairs, she called Maddie and apologized. Of course, there was no need to do so, as Maddie had already forgiven her.

Children's voices could be heard in the background and Sky was delighted her sister was as happy as happy could be.

"Kira wants to play with Georgie. Can we set up a playdate?"

"Sure. I'll call you as soon as I know what my day is going to be like."

As Sky reached the bottom of the stairs, she heard rain pelting the windows. *Oh, no.* The weather affected Kira more than anything, but she had seemed fine this morning.

Sky hurriedly made her way to the kitchen, to find her daughter still yakking with Gran. But that didn't necessarily mean she wasn't in pain.

Don't ask! Don't ask!

Kira glanced up with a childish smile that melted Sky's heart. Her baby turned up her palms. "Oatmeal all gone, Mommy. Now can I play with Georgie?"

"Aunt Maddie will call." Sky scooped her out of the chair. "Time to get you dressed." She'd been planning to ask Gran to do that, but now she wanted to check Kira's joints.

Upstairs, she removed Kira's princess pj's, finding her right knee still red and slightly swollen. After dressing her in jeans, a T-shirt and sneakers, Sky gave her some liquid Tylenol. As Kira bounced down the stairs, Sky wondered if that might have been a waste. Kira didn't seem to be in pain, but on a day like this she couldn't be sure.

In the parlor, she brushed her daughter's hair into pigtails. Looking at Kira's pixie face, Sky thought her baby had to be the cutest on the planet—the way every mother felt.

"Precious, Mommy's going to work and you're staying with Gran and Etta, okay?"

"Uh-huh."

She kissed her nose. "You be good."

"I be good." Kira twisted her hands. "Is Georgie coming?"

Goodness gracious, the kid had a memory like an elephant. When the two had first met, Georgie had taken an instant dislike to Kira because Maddie was holding her. Once he realized Kira had a mother and wasn't trying to steal his, they became good friends.

"I'll call Aunt Maddie a little later."

"Where's my precious baby?" Gran called as she entered the room.

"I'm here," Kira shouted.

Sky walked to Gran as Kira opened her case of Barbies. "Call me if you feel something is wrong. I'll have my cell with me at all times."

Her grandmother pushed her toward the door. "Go, and stop worrying."

Sky grabbed a lightweight windbreaker on her way out. Flipping the hood over her head, she made a dash for the barn. She almost made it before Solomon blocked her path. The half-Brahman bull's mother had died, and Cait and Maddie had raised him on a bottle.

He was now a huge pet—and a pest. Sky worried about Kira being around him, but Georgie loved him and led the bull around like a dog. Since Georgie was Kira's hero, she followed him everywhere. It was almost impossible to keep her from doing things Georgie did. Solomon was a lovable creature, though, and hard to resist.

Rain peppered Sky's face as she grabbed his halter. "Come on. I'll feed you."

Cooper and Rufus were in the barn, and they stilled as she entered with Solomon trailing behind her.

She tossed back her hood. "Morning."

Rufus removed his hat and scratched his thinning gray hair. "Girl, this ain't a day for you to be out."

She placed her hands on her hips. "Now, Ru, that sounds just like my dad."

"Maybe he had a point."

"I don't think so. I run this ranch now and I will be involved in every aspect of it."

"Mmm." Ru mulled that over. Cooper was in the background, straightening bridles on the wall. In keeping with his infuriating habit, he didn't look her way. "We were going to change the oil in the tractors and baling equipment, so we'd be ready for harvesting season."

"That's a good idea." She glanced outside at the rain making puddles in the dirt. "Don't know how long this is going to last, so let's get started."

Cooper glanced up, his eyes narrowed beneath the brim of his hat. "Do you even know how to change oil?"

She bit her lip. "Yes, I do." Being on her own, she'd learned to do a lot of things, including changing the oil in her car. It was much cheaper. And she'd seen Cait changing the oil in the tractors, so she knew she could do it.

Solomon, tired of waiting, butted her. Not hard, just enough to let her know he was still hungry.

"Okay." She took his halter. "I'll feed you."

"I've already fed him," Cooper said in an icy voice.

His tone irritated her. Well, everything about him irritated her. "He's still hungry."

"He's always hungry." The statement was just as frigid as his first response.

"I'll give him a little something to appease him."

"Suit yourself. You're the boss."

She lifted an eyebrow. "I'm glad we've settled that."

She waited for a retort, but none came. With a frown deep enough to hold water, he strolled to the door that led to the lean-to equipment shed.

She stuck out her tongue at his back. *Damn*. She couldn't help it.

Shaking his head, Ru followed Cooper. She reached for a galvanized bucket and went into the supply room for sweet feed. Solomon followed her to the trough under the overhang of the barn, and she dumped the feed into it.

Rushing back, she grabbed a pair of denim overalls from a hook. They were Cait's, and Sky knew she used them for dirty jobs. She slipped into them and quickly joined Rufus and Cooper.

Several tractors and other pieces of equipment were parked in the lean-to. Ru was working on the hay baler, while Cooper squatted and looked at the underbelly of a John Deere.

She knew she was going to have to prove herself. Another thing that irritated her, but she was trying to be nice and get along. A little cooperation on Yates's part wouldn't kill him.

"I'll change this one," she said.

He stood and they were inches apart. A woodsy

outdoor scent tickled her nose and a long-forgotten heat tempted her senses. Golden curls of hair peeped out of the V in his western shirt. He was too close for comfort. Too close without touching…Was she insane? This man hated her and she'd do well to remember that.

"By all means."

Cooper tried not to look at her in the overalls, but he failed. He didn't want to notice one thing about her, but her fair, clean skin, devoid of makeup, was a shock. That host of freckles spread across a pert nose was hard to miss, as were the curves of her body outlined by the denim. How did she manage to look sexy in those things?

"What do you put the old oil in?" she asked.

He pointed to a five-gallon bucket and a funnel, but made no move to hand it to her. That wasn't like him. He helped Cait and Maddie all the time, but with her…

She reached for a crescent wrench from the toolbox on the ground and pulled the bucket forward as if she knew what she was doing. *This could be entertaining,* he thought, stepping back.

Locating the drain plug on the underside of the cylinder block, she applied the wrench. No luck. The plug was tight with grease and gunk.

The pouring rain hammered the tin roof of the lean-to with a soothing metallic rhythm as she worked on the plug. Suddenly, it popped free and dirty oil squirted everywhere. On the ground. On the tractor. On her.

With a quick reflex, Coop shoved the bucket forward to catch the oil. Oil splattered her face, her overalls and her hair. She looked shocked and he wanted to laugh. He didn't. Instead he handed her an old rag.

She pushed herself to her feet, wiped her face and then made sure the bucket was still catching the dripping oil.

"I'll finish," he offered, for no other reason than to get rid of her.

"I can finish it." She rubbed oil from her cheek, only managing to smear it. He thought she'd go running to the house, since the girl he'd briefly known wouldn't get her hands dirty. Had she changed?

He knew she had a child; he'd seen the little girl playing in the yard. But there wasn't a husband. Seeing her as a mother was a stretch. Seeing her as a responsible, caring woman was a stretch. Seeing her as much of anything besides a social piranha was an even bigger stretch.

And he was being judgmental—like so many people had treated him. He'd sworn he'd never do that. But with her…

"Thank you." She handed him the rag, and he looked at this woman with the oil-smeared face. Why did he hate her? She really had nothing to do with his situation. She'd only been a bystander.

Keeping up this barrage of anger was eating at him. She was Dane's daughter, and Coop had to shake whatever was driving him. Taking the rag, he turned and hurried into the barn.

He whistled for Rebel and the horse responded, galloping into the corral, his coat wet. In a matter of minutes, Coop was saddled up and bolted out into rain, needing to put distance between them.

The rain stopped after lunch, but still he didn't return. He would finish the tractors that evening. Most nights he didn't sleep, anyway.

He blocked out thoughts of her and concentrated on the ranch. The rain was good for the corn and the hay-fields, as long as they didn't get too much. If that happened, he'd have to figure out some sort of drainage. One way or another, High Five was going to have a successful crop this year.

Old boards tossed into the grass by the side of the main house caught his attention. He dismounted to check them out. They'd probably been blown around by the hurricane that had come through last September.

Squatting, he saw it was an old hand-dug well shaft, abandoned years ago. He picked up the boards. A cow could step in the hole and break a leg. Tomorrow he'd fill it up with dirt. That would be the safest way to avoid any injuries.

He used one of the small boards to scoop out indentation to lay the boards in so the wind couldn't move them. He then kicked dirt on top with his boot. That would do for now.

Darkness fell like a heavy cloak, the moon hidden beneath its folds. He headed for the barn and rubbed Rebel down and fed him. The dogs whined at him, not liking that he'd left them behind.

Stepping out of the barn, Coop saw the lights were on at the house, but he didn't turn in that direction. He marched purposefully toward the bunkhouse, his private space.

First, he fed the dogs and played with them for a while. They licked his face and wagged their tails, forgiving easily. He needed to find that emotion somewhere inside him.

His clothes were still damp, so he took a quick shower. Drying off, he heard a knock—no doubt Rufus, bringing supper. Coop grabbed jeans and hopped, skipped and jumped into them as he made his way toward the door. He'd have to tell Ru to stop bringing food. He could cook his own meals.

In the hallway, he shouted, "Come in."

Sky opened the door, to find the dogs looking at her with an expectant gaze.

She forgot about them as soon as she saw Coop standing in the doorway, buttoning his jeans. And that was all he had on. His blond hair was wet from the shower and tousled across his forehead. Tiny beads of water glistened on his shoulders. A wide span of chest was covered in golden hairs that disappeared into his jeans. Her heart rate kicked into overdrive at the sight of him.

She must have been without a man too long. She wasn't attracted to Cooper Yates. Was she?

He yanked a T-shirt from a chair and jerked it over his head. The muscles in his arms bulged from the movement. *Oh, yeah. That helped to ease the tension. Not.*

Focus.

For a split second Sky was caught by the simplicity of the bunkhouse. Years ago the sisters' teenage curiosity had gotten the best of them, and they'd sneaked in to get a peek at where the cowboys lived. Of course, they were caught, and their father was not pleased. After a stern lecture, they promised never, ever to be so bold or so foolish again. Maddie was the only one who'd paid attention.

The bunkhouse was the same as it had been back then. Hardwood flooring worn by years of cowboys boot-scooting across it. Dark paneled walls. A large living area—kitchen combo highlighted with a huge stone fireplace charred by use. The hallway led to two oversize bedrooms that slept eight cowboys each. A bath separated the rooms.

"Nothing fancy—just a place to live." Her father had said that many times.

What surprised Sky was the computer sitting on a small desk. And the TV in front of a recliner. All the comforts of home—Cooper's home.

The warm plate in her hand reminded her she was standing there staring like that teenage girl of long ago. She walked over and set the plate on the homemade wooden table.

"I brought your supper, and for the record, this will be the last time anyone brings you food unless you're sick. Even if you don't care about anyone else, please respect my grandmother's wishes and eat at the house."

He just stared at her and then said, "You got the oil out of your hair."

"What? Oh. Yes." Her hand went to the freshly washed curls around her face. "It boggles my mind the tricks Etta knows to remove stains. I've never had my hair washed with Lava soap."

He just kept staring.

"In case you're wondering, running away didn't help a thing. Rufus and I changed the oil and filters in every tractor."

"No kidding."

"No kidding," she shot back.

Silence intruded and she thought it was time for her to leave. She'd said what she'd needed to. But being a true Belle, she could never leave well enough alone. "Are we clear on the meals thing?"

"Yes, ma'am."

She wanted to smack those words back at him, but instead, she turned to walk out the door. Since throwing caution to the wind seemed to be her trademark, she pivoted and said, "I'm not leaving this room until you tell me why you don't like me."

He took a step toward her, the green of his eyes overshadowed by some dark emotions. "You don't remember, do you?"

"Remember? Have I met you before?" She couldn't have. She wouldn't have forgotten someone like him.

"Yes. Several times."

Shocked, she gaped at him. "Where? When?"

"The name Everett Coleman ring a bell?"

A sliver of alarm slithered up her spine. "Of course, he was my mother's fifth husband."

"Four years ago I was his foreman at the Rocking C Thoroughbred Farms."

"What?" Suddenly she couldn't breathe.

"Everett Coleman was the man who framed me."

CHAPTER FOUR

"WHAT?"

"While your mother lived at the Rocking C, you came many times to visit, usually with a couple of friends in tow."

"Yes, but I don't remember seeing you." Her voice came out hoarse, and she curled her hands into fists.

"The cowboys and I were hired hands, and beneath you and your friends. You mostly made fun of us and called us names."

She swallowed a wad of guilt that haunted her from those years—years of rebellion, years of living life on the edge. How did she explain that to him? How did she admit she had been a pampered, spoiled bitch?

Her throat worked but no words came out.

"You and your friends spent the afternoons around the pool in skimpy bikinis, leaving the privacy gate open so the cowboys could see. At night y'all hit the clubs in Fort Worth. One night y'all came in around 3:00 a.m. I was checking a mare that was about to foal. You were trying to put a saddle on Juniper Rose, and I told you no way were you going to ride that horse. You were drunk out of your mind. You gave me a tongue-lashing I won't soon forget, but I refused to let you ride the horse. You told me to pack my things because I wouldn't have a job in the morning."

Sky felt color stain her cheeks. She remembered. Oh, God! She hated going to the Rocking C, but her mother had whined and whined until she'd given in. Sky had always taken friends with her to get through the weekend. And they did what rich girls did best—they partied.

"The next morning Everett said you were leaving that afternoon, and to make myself invisible until then. Ol' Everett had a plan and nothing was getting in the way of it, including you." Coop's eyes bored into her. "I spent six months in a Huntsville prison because of him."

"I'm sorry. I really am, but I had nothing to do with that."

"I know," he admitted, to her surprise. "But women like you and your mother, who drive men to do the unspeakable, rub me the wrong way."

She licked her suddenly dry lips. "I'm not my mother and I'm not the same woman you met on that ranch."

His eyes swept over her and a chill ran through her. "You look the same."

"Really?" She lifted an eyebrow. "My hair is frizzed out. I'm not wearing makeup, and I have oil on my boots and on my jeans. Not to mention I'm broke. I'm hardly that self-centered, tongue-lashing bitch you met."

"Maybe." He folded his arms across his chest. "It's hard for me to believe you're Dane's daughter. Cait and Maddie are so loving and caring. As a boy, I wanted to run away many times, but I stayed and finished high school because of Cait. She never gave up on me. And Maddie...well, she's the nicest person I've ever met."

"And I'm the bitch."

His eyes met hers. "If you say so."

"I don't." She straightened her backbone, determined

to tell her side. "Motherhood has changed me. Back then I hated all the glitz and glamour of the Rocking C, and I especially disliked my mother's husband. I suppose I felt if I rebelled enough, Mom would stop insisting that I visit. My life wasn't as much fun as you might think, but I'm not going to stand here and try to explain my past behavior. I'm sorry for what was done to you by Everett. He's a scumbag. But hating me is not going to help our situation here at High Five. That's my concern now."

Coop unfolded his arms, his eyes still holding hers with that sizzling glare. "You think you can work with an ex-con?"

"Yes." Her eyes didn't waver from the challenge in his. She took a step closer. "Cait says this ranch can't survive without you. We can either see if that's true or we can make High Five a prosperous operation once again."

He didn't move or speak, but the muscles in his arms worked from clenching his hands.

"Cait's always talking about the bottom line. Well, this is it. We can either be friends or enemies—your choice." Sky paused and then added, "Ru said I needed to give you a chance. That works both ways. I can't change the past, but I can make the future better."

On that, she walked out the door and didn't bother to close it. Once she reached the edge of the lighted area, she bolted through the darkness. Her lungs tight, she sank to the ground beneath an oak tree.

Life was hell when you had to look at yourself through a two-way mirror and see all your faults and bad habits in living color. Pointed out by a man who had been on the receiving end of her bad behavior. She never dreamed she'd met him before. She'd never... Damn it! She could blame a lot of people, but the only person to blame was herself. Back then her resentment toward her mother had clouded her judgment and her actions. Sky had been out of control, drinking and partying way too much.

Drawing a long breath, she listened to the coyotes in the distance and the crickets chirping. *She was wrong*. She'd misjudged Cooper because he hadn't been bowled over by her. That's what had irritated her. Seeing vanity in herself wasn't easy.

Cait had always said that one day Sky might have to eat her words about Cooper. She was, and they tasted like a bull nettle going down her throat. Startling. Burning. Awakening.

She glanced up toward the heavens. "If you're watching, I could use a little help." Her father had said that when she was grown she would see her faults clearly. They were about as bright as the twinkling stars. She rose to her feet and started toward the house.

Growing up was hell.

COOPER STOOD THERE for five minutes before he closed the door. He hadn't meant to say so much, but she had a way of triggering his emotions. He didn't analyze that any further because he didn't want to know why the woman had such an effect on him. Never in his life had he judged anyone, but with her he couldn't help himself.

He sat at the table and pushed the plate aside.

Friends or enemies.

His choice.

There was only one way to settle this, the same way he settled every big decision in his life. He never thought of himself as a gambler, but some days a man just had to take a risk.

Jamming a hand into his jeans pocket, he pulled out a quarter. As he flipped it in the air, he called, "Heads." Catching the coin, he laid it flat on the table and stared at it a long time. "That's the way it will be." He blew out a breath. "And God help us all."

COOPER WOKE UP at 4:00 a.m., as always. He had an internal clock that never failed him. After making coffee, he dressed. The food the redhead had brought still sat on the table. It was ruined now, so he carried it outside and gave it to the dogs. Then he washed the plate and drank two cups of coffee. Ready for the day, he headed for the barn, keeping his mind blank. He refused to think about the redhead.

He walked to the lean-to and crawled onto a tractor with a front-end loader. The open well shaft he'd found yesterday had to be filled. The tractor puttered to life and he could see clearly in the beam of the headlights. An hour later he had the hole filled with sand. He laid the boards back on top and dumped more sand to make them secure. Now he felt sure the problem was solved.

Driving back, he saw a group of wild pigs scurrying away from the tractor. Damn! They could do more damage than good to the pastures.

As he parked the tractor in the lean-to, he knew he couldn't hold off the morning. And his decision.

A yellow glow already bathed the sky, and soon the sun would burst forth to start another day. A peaceful quiet seemed to prevail before the world awoke. He felt that quiet inside him, urging him on. He headed for the house.

As he entered the kitchen, Etta was at the stove and Ru sat eating breakfast.

Etta glanced at him. "It's about time. Have a seat. I'll have your breakfast ready in no time."

"Thank you, Etta." He placed his hat on a rack.

Sitting next to Ru, he avoided looking at the little girl seated across the table in a booster chair.

"Glad you and Sky got everything sorted out," Rufus said, buttering a biscuit.

Coop didn't answer as he accepted the mug of coffee Etta handed him.

"I'm Kira," a little voice said from across the table.

Cooper didn't know a thing about kids so he thought it best to ignore the child.

"What's your name?"

He took a swallow of coffee.

"What's your name?" the kid persisted.

"For Pete's sake, answer," Ru snapped.

Coop looked at the little girl with the red curly hair. Dressed in a pink nightgown, she held an orangey-red stuffed animal in one arm.

Swallowing, he said, "I'm Cooper."

"Coo."

"Cooper."

"Coo."

"Coop…"

He trailed off as Etta placed bacon and eggs in front of him.

"What you eating, Coo?"

Cooper clenched his jaw. Did the kid have a hearing problem? "Bacon and eggs," he muttered, hoping the little girl turned her attention elsewhere.

"Etta, can I have bacon and eggs, please?"

"You haven't finished your oatmeal."

"I don't like it."

"Mmm. You'll eat bacon and eggs?"

"Yes."

Coop dug into his breakfast and did his best to ignore the child.

"I played with Georgie yesterday. He's having a birthday party and I'm going."

Coop took a bite of biscuit and kept on ignoring her.

"I think it's tomorrow. I don't know. I have to ask Mommy, but Aunt Maddie's making a cake and everything. Do you like cake?"

Coop took another swallow of coffee.

Rufus stood with his plate in his hand. Bending low, he whispered, "She's not contagious."

"Yeah," Coop mumbled.

Etta laid a small plate with a cut-up egg and some bacon in front of the girl. The child picked up a fork and began to eat. Coop noticed her watching him. Every time he put a bite in his mouth, so did she. When he reached for his coffee, she drank her milk.

The redhead appeared in the doorway, dressed for the day in tight jeans and a pearl-snap shirt that outlined her curvy breasts. Not that he noticed.

The child swung to her. "Look, Mommy, I'm eating with Coo."

Sky glanced from her child to him. "You ate eggs?"

The girl nodded, sporting a milk mustache.

"Time to get dressed, baby."

Cooper rose to his feet, banking down any resentment he felt toward this woman. "I thought I'd check the hayfields this morning to see how much rain we got. As soon as it dries out, we should be able to get a first cutting."

Sky did a double take. His voice sounded cordial.

Almost. But she wasn't going to look this gift horse in the mouth. He was here, eating. That was a step forward.

"Good," she replied.

"I saw some wild pigs this morning and I want to make sure they're not rooting up the fields."

"Wild pigs?"

"They're common around here."

"Yeah." Rufus joined the conversation. "Skully Lutz traps them. I can give him a call if you want."

"What does he charge?" Sky asked.

"Nothing. He just keeps all the pigs he catches."

She looked at Cooper. "Do you think it's a good idea to call him?"

"It couldn't hurt. They travel in groups and they could really damage our hayfields. Our pastures, too."

"Then call, Ru. We don't need anything else working against us."

"Will do."

Both men ambled toward the back door.

"Coo," Kira called.

Cooper stopped in his tracks and slowly glanced back.

"Bye." Kira smiled.

He nodded, grabbed his hat and was gone.

Sky suppressed a grin. Evidently Cooper was a little nervous around children. But her daughter had a way of working magic.

"Come on, baby. Mommy has to get you dressed. I have to go to work."

"I can dress myself."

"Really?"

"Yes." Kira crawled from the chair with Sky's help. "I'm big like Georgie and Coo."

Cooper was in a whole different ballpark than

Georgie, but obviously Kira saw them as strong hero types.

"Miss Dorie and I will help her," Etta said. "You better go or you'll never find Ru and Coop."

"Thanks, Etta." Sky bent low to kiss her child. "Mommy will be back later."

"'Kay."

"Etta…"

"I have your cell number. Stop worrying."

She grabbed a worn felt hat as Etta and Kira walked out, the little girl chattering nonstop. Sky and her baby had been together so much Sky thought Kira would miss her. But Kira was social and adaptable to every situation, much like her mother.

So many times during her youth, Sky had had to adjust to new living arrangements, a new home, a new stepfather, but she never did it with as much grace as Kira. Sky tended to pout and rebel. She prayed that part of her nature was gone forever.

She hurried out the door to start this new phase of her life. She was going to be so damn agreeable, Cooper Yates wasn't going to know what hit him.

THE DAY WENT BETTER than Sky had hoped. Cooper didn't ignore her, but she felt her presence was a strain on him. Yet they were trying. That was the important part.

The ranch had gotten two inches of rain, so the crops were thriving. A week of sunshine and they could start cutting hay for baling.

At noon they went back to the house for lunch. Kira and Gran were having a tea party in the parlor around the coffee table. Kira wore a hat with faded satin ribbons and feathers, definitely from the forties as was Gran's.

"We're having camel tea, Mommy," Kira said, lifting a cup to her mouth with her little pinkie stuck out.

"Camel tea?"

"Chamomile, my baby," Gran corrected her.

"Yeah, that."

They were having fun so Sky left, feeling better about being away from her daughter.

That afternoon she, Rufus and Cooper rode through the herd. They stopped putting out feed long ago, since there was plenty of green grass. Toward the woods, they could see buzzards circling.

Cooper pulled up the paint. "Let's hope that's a dead squirrel or a raccoon."

Sky and Ru followed as he steered the paint into the woods.

"Son of a bitch." Cooper swung from the horse and ran to the black cow stretched out on the ground. A baby calf's feet protruded from her rear end.

Coop knelt by the cow and she didn't move. "Damn it! I knew this heifer was fixing to calve, and I was keeping a close watch on her. With the rain and all, I didn't check her last night."

Sky knelt beside him. "Is she dead?"

"No, but she might as well be." He removed his hat and swiped an arm across his forehead.

"Isn't there something we can do?"

Cooper ran his hand over the cow's swollen stomach and studied the unborn calf. "First, we have to get this out of her. It's dead. No telling how long she's been out here like this. Damn it! *Damn* it!" He stood and marched to his horse, grabbing a rope. "We have to pull the calf."

Sky didn't say anything, because this was something

she knew nothing about. She had a feeling she was going to get a lesson in ranching today.

From a man who wished she was anywhere but here.

CHAPTER FIVE

COOPER STUDIED THE CALF once again.

"What's the plan, boy?" Ru asked.

"Both feet and head are in the right position. My guess is the calf was too big for her to have and must have died during the struggle of birthing." Coop looped the rope around both its hooves and tied a knot. "You and I have to pull it."

"Can I help?" Sky asked.

"Try to keep the heifer calm."

"How do I do that?"

"Use your instincts," he snapped.

If she was a whiny female, that just might have hurt her feelings. But she'd show Mr. Yates.

He strolled to his horse and rummaged in his saddlebags, returning with a tube of something. Squirting what looked like a lubricant into his palm, he rubbed it over both hands.

Sky knelt in the patchy grass at the heifer's head. The cow made a deep guttural sound and her big brown eyes seemed to say, *Help me*.

Sky swallowed hard. Clearly the heifer was in pain. She stroked the animal's neck, and glanced to see if Coop was making any progress.

With his hands lubricated, he stuck one inside the

cow, likely checking on the positioning of the calf, Sky guessed. The heifer jerked, trying to get to her feet.

"Whoa, girl. Calm down." Sky stroked her soothingly.

"The calf is in the right position, as I thought. She just couldn't birth it. We have to pull," Coop said to Ru.

Both men grabbed the rope-tied legs.

"Yank out and down," Coop said as they worked. "Pull, Ru. It's coming. I can feel it. One more tug." The calf slid out, along with blood and yellow mucous, and the heifer made a gut-wrenching sound.

"Thank God." Coop sat back on his heels for a second, then placed his hand over the calf's mouth. "It's dead."

"And the heifer's in bad shape," Ru commented.

Cooper turned his attention to the cow, running his hands over her legs and back. "Son of a bitch! She's paralyzed."

"We'll have to shoot her." Ru shook his head.

"What?" Sky was aghast.

Ru looked at her. "That's what we do with animals like this."

"Isn't there another way?" She knew her feminine side was showing, but she couldn't help it.

"Her back end is paralyzed. She can't stand. You might want to go back to the house."

"I will not."

"Girl…"

"*Is* there another way? That's all I'm asking."

Rufus glanced at Cooper, who wiped his forehead again. "There's a slim chance, but it takes a lot of time and work. With the hay and corn season upon us, we don't have time. It might not work, anyway."

Sky stroked the animal and looked at those brown eyes. "What is it?"

He sighed deeply.

"I'll do it, whatever it is."

"It takes more than one person."

Rufus walked toward his horse, and Sky knew he was getting his rifle.

"We're not shooting this heifer," she said loudly so Ru could hear her. Then she glanced at Cooper. "What do we do?"

"She isn't a person, you know."

"What do we *do?*"

"For starters, we have to get her back to the barn. Then we put her in a harness so we can raise her a couple of times a day. That way she can try to use her muscles to stand. But she may not regain feeling in her legs. It's a gamble."

Sky stood and straightened her shoulders. "I'm taking it. Let's get her back to the ranch."

Cooper turned away and she thought she heard a cussword. She wasn't giving in, though.

Two hours later they had the heifer in the barn. It had taken a flatbed trailer, ropes and a lot of muscle, but the heifer was now lying in a horse stall. Both men seemed ticked off at Sky, but she held her ground.

After supper, she followed Cooper to the barn.

"I can make the harness by myself," he said over his shoulder.

"I know, but since this was my idea I need to do as much as I can."

"That would have been about four hours ago."

"Sorry. I'm not going to kill her when there's a chance to save her."

"You're the boss."

"And don't forget it."

The corners of his mouth twitched. Was he trying hard not to smile? Impossible. A smile would crack his face.

Rufus had gone to the general store for some heavy canvas material, which turned out to be an old-fashioned cotton sack about twenty feet long. Cooper sat on a bench and used his pocket knife to cut two holes on each end.

His hands were strong and sure, the sculpted lines of his face intense. She had a feeling he did everything with that same concentration, and with a capability she'd never noticed before.

Beads of perspiration popped out on his upper lip, which was dark with a five o'clock shadow. She studied his mouth. It was as sculpted as his face, and his lower lip curved with a hint of sensuality. As a warmth centered in her lower abdomen, she had the urge to wipe the sweat away—with her tongue.

She swallowed hard.

"This will cradle her stomach much like a sling cradles an arm," he said, cutting off the strap that would go over a person's shoulder. "We insert ropes here—" he pointed to the holes "—and attach them to a pulley and another rope, which will go over the rafters. With a little muscle, we can raise her to her feet."

"Ingenious."

He stared into Sky's eyes and couldn't believe her enthusiasm. He'd gone along with her plan, thinking she'd tire of it eventually, but he had a feeling she was genuinely sincere. The girl he'd met on the Rocking C wouldn't care two bits for this paralyzed cow. Had she changed?

When he had the ropes tied in place, she asked, "Now what?"

"We get this cradle beneath the heifer." He rose from the workbench. "How strong are you?"

"Why?"

"The heifer is deadweight and we have to get this under her."

"Oh. Just tell me what to do."

Leave me in peace.

He shook off the thought and strolled to the stall. Straddling the cow, he said, "When I lift her, shove one end, ropes and all, beneath her as fast as you can. I'm not Hercules."

"Got it." She knelt in the straw and positioned the sack and ropes as far under the cow's belly as she could. The animal gave a low bellow.

"Ready?"

"Yes."

Slowly, Coop took a deep breath and lifted with all his strength. The cow's belly rose about an inch, and Sky shoved and jammed with lightning speed.

His muscles protested in pain and he swung away, flexing his arms. "Damn. She's heavier than I thought."

Sky sat back on her heels, her eyes shining. "Oh, please, that was a piece of cake for you." She paused. "Hercules."

He stared into those blue depths and found he was lost. Totally and completely lost in whatever spell she was weaving. Cait and Maddie had the same blue eyes, but the redhead's were different. They were playful, teasing, coaxing. He felt as if he was lying in the grass on a summer day and staring into the bluest sky he'd ever seen—a blue that went on forever, soothing, beguiling and pulling him so far into a vortex of…

He blinked and knelt, attaching ropes to a pulley with strong jerks. She wouldn't get to him.

For the next fifteen minutes they worked in silence. He liked it that way. Climbing the gate of the stall, he managed to throw the big rope over a rafter. After that, he drove a spike into a post to anchor it once the cow was lifted.

He wiped his dusty hands on his jeans. "When Ru gets here, we'll try to hoist her to her feet."

Sky stared at him. "You have a spiderweb entangled in your hair."

Running both hands through his hair, he said, "Those damn things are everywhere."

"You still didn't get it."

"They stick like glue."

She reached up and gently removed the web, and a faint whiff of sweat and dust mingled with the scent of her. It permeated his nostrils, then settled in his chest and kept company with the pounding of his heart. He had to take a breath.

"Thanks."

"No problem." She glanced at the prone heifer. "I really appreciate what you're doing."

Rufus entered the barn and all Cooper could think was *thank God*. Being alone with her was taking more strength than lifting the heifer.

"I finally got the vet. He'll be here in a few minutes."

"Good." Coop nodded. "He needs to check her before we go any further."

"I have to get Kira ready for bed. I'll be right back," Sky said.

She made a dash for the house, needing some breathing space. She'd been around a lot of men, but none made her feel sixteen and breathless by just watching them.

Kira and Gran were in the parlor on the sofa, playing with the dolls. Kira's tongue was clenched between her teeth as she tugged a skirt on one.

"Time for bed, precious," Sky said.

"I don't want to." Her daughter never looked up as she reached for a blouse. "Gran and me are playing."

"Kira…"

"I'll put her to bed," Gran offered. "Go take care of the cow. Kira and I will be fine."

"Are you sure?" Her grandmother had changed so much in the months that Sky had been home. The sadness in her eyes wasn't so prevalent and she smiled more. Coming home had been the right decision, for all of them.

"Yes, my baby," Gran replied. "Now go."

Sky turned toward the door, knowing her daughter was in good hands.

"Mommy?" Kira called.

She turned back. "What, precious?"

"Is tomorrow Georgie's birthday party?"

"Yes, it is."

"I'm gonna wear my pretty blue shorts and sandals."

"Fine."

"And this hat." Kira picked up Gran's old hat with the ribbons and feathers.

"Kira, that's to play in."

"I know." She plopped it on her head.

"We'll talk about it later. Mommy has to go."

"'Kay."

Sky hurried out the door. Hopefully, by tomorrow Kira would forget about the hat. But her kid had some memory.

As she reached the barn, she saw a white truck with

toolboxes on both sides of the bed parked outside. It had to be the vet's.

A man of medium height, wearing a straw hat, stepped out of the truck. She guessed he must be in his sixties. "Ms. Belle?" he asked when he spotted her.

"I'm Skylar Belle."

"Charlie Paxton, the vet." He held out his hand and she shook it. "I heard the youngest Belle daughter was now running High Five."

"Yes. I'm home to stay."

He tipped back his hat. "Seems kind of strange for a pretty woman like you to be running a ranch." Before she could get in a word, he added, "Now, I would never say that to Caitlyn. She'd take a strip off my hide a mile wide."

"You might want to think twice before saying it to me. My temper is as red-hot as my hair."

He pulled his hat low. "Yes, ma'am."

Idiot.

He reached inside the cab for a black bag. "Now, ma'am, I don't mean to upset you, but I'd just as soon not work with Cooper Yates."

"Excuse me?"

"I'm an animal lover and I know he was cleared of the charges for killing those horses, but there's still the doubt."

"I suggest you take that doubt and stuff it where the sun don't shine. Cooper Yates works on this ranch and we're trying to save a heifer. I could use your help, not your narrow-minded bigotry."

He didn't say another word as he followed her into the barn.

Oh, God. Cait was right. Guilt beat at Sky like a persistent headache. She could see herself so clearly in Mr. Paxton. She hadn't given Cooper a chance, just like everyone else in this town. The two-way mirror was working overtime.

As the vet entered the stall, Cooper moved away. He stood just outside, watching while Charlie knelt in the straw and examined the heifer.

"She's paralyzed," he concluded. "I can put her to sleep or you can shoot her."

"I'm trying to prevent those things, Mr. Paxton."

He leaned back on his heels. "It's a waste of time. This heifer will be dead in less than a week."

She noticed Cooper whispering to Rufus.

"Cooper, did you have something to say?" She wasn't going to let him cater to this man's bigotry.

"She might need antibiotics to stave off infection, and high-dose vitamin shots to build her strength."

"It's a waste of money." The vet got to his feet.

Sky stared directly at him. "For a man who loves animals you're very quick to kill this cow."

Color swept under his skin. "Fine. I have antibiotics and vitamins in my truck, but they're not cheap."

"I didn't expect them to be."

The vet went to his vehicle and she dashed to the house for a check. He had a bill waiting when she returned. Sky didn't quibble about the price; she just wanted to get rid of the man.

As she handed him the check, she said, "Stop by in a month and you'll see the heifer will still be living."

"I saw the harness and all. I guess you're planning to lift her every day."

"Yes. I'm going to give that heifer every chance. That's what loving animals means."

"It means a loss in time and money, and it's no way to run a ranch."

"I think you better leave before I really get angry."

He inclined his head, got in his truck and drove away.

"Bastard," she said under her breath.

"Still using those bad words."

Sky jumped at Ru's comment. "Sometimes I just can't help it."

"Me, neither," he whispered with a rare smile. "Well, it's after nine, and my bedtime. See you in the morning, girl."

Sky made her way back into the barn. Cooper was kneeling in the hay with a syringe in his hand. And the heifer's head was up.

Sinking into the hay, she exclaimed, "She's better."

"She's hungry."

"I'll get her some feed."

"Bring her some water first."

The cow drank thirstily from the bucket and Sky rushed to get her some sweet feed. Cooper injected two shots into her hip.

After eating, the animal struggled to get to her feet. As she jerked and twisted, Cooper said, "That's a problem. She's going to hurt herself struggling." He stood. "I'll look in the supply room. Cait used to keep tranquilizers for Whiskey Red. The horse was very temperamental and I'm assuming still is."

"If we don't have any, I'll call Cait."

He walked to the supply room and in a minute was back with a small vial. "We're in luck." He injected the heifer once again and in a few minutes she settled down. "Now we'll let her get some rest, and in the morning we'll try the harness."

As they headed for the door, Sky asked, "Where's Solomon?"

"I put him in the pen next to the corral to keep him out of the way."

"Good idea."

Cooper flicked off the barn light and they stepped out into the darkness.

"I heard what you said to Paxton."

She turned to face him, the moonlight casting an iridescent glow around them. "I meant it."

"I heard it with my own ears, and I'm still finding it hard to believe."

"Cait has often said that I'm an ass, and I really hate admitting she's right, but in this case she is. I was narrow-minded and judgmental, just like Charlie Paxton."

"What changed your mind?"

"You. You care about High Five just as much as we do, and you care for every animal on this property. Even Ru wouldn't help me with the heifer, but you did." Sky tucked a stray curl behind her ear. "I'm sorry for the way I treated you."

The apology hung between them for long moments. "Thanks," he finally said, his voice husky.

There was a slight hesitation in his voice and she had the feeling he didn't want to say her name.

"My name is Skylar."

He rocked back on his heels. "I think I'll call you Red."

"Red? That's Cait's horse!"

"It fits. You're both temperamental."

She placed her hands on her hips. "You will not call me Red."

He tipped his hat. "'Night, Red."

As he disappeared into the darkness, a smile spread across her face. The name had never sounded so good.

CHAPTER SIX

THE NEXT MORNING Sky was up early. She dressed and took Kira down for breakfast.

"Good morning, ladies," Etta said. "What would you like to eat?"

Sky poured milk for Kira. "How about cereal, precious?"

"No." Her daughter shook her head, her red curls bobbing. "I want bacon and eggs like Coo." Sky could never get her to eat eggs before, and now she wanted them because Cooper ate them?

"Coming right up," Etta said.

"Thanks. I'm going to the barn to see how the heifer is doing." She turned toward the door. "Kira, Mommy will be right back."

"I'll watch her until Miss Dorie gets up," the housekeeper offered.

"Gran was still asleep when I checked on her."

"She'll be up soon," Etta replied. "She's not going to miss a minute of caring for Kira. It's been the best medicine in the world for her."

Sky hurried out the door and ran to the barn, eager to see how the cow was faring. She stopped short in the doorway. Cooper was already there, with a tractor backed up to the stall.

"What are you doing?" she asked as he jumped off the vehicle. Even from a few feet away, she could feel the power of him, and it did a number on her senses.

"The tranquilizer has worn off and the heifer is agitated again. I have the harness all rigged up. It's time to lift her."

"With the tractor, huh?"

"It'll be a lot easier on my muscles." He glanced up. "I'm hoping those rafters will hold."

"What can I do?"

"Say a prayer that it works."

"Got that covered."

He paused in tying the rope to the hitch, his green eyes sparkling. "Never figured you for a praying woman."

"I have all kinds of secrets," she whispered, and realized she was flirting. Some habits were hard to break.

He tightened the knot with a grin. "Now, let's see what happens." Crawling onto the tractor, he said, "Stand back in case the rafters break."

She prayed they wouldn't.

The tractor sputtered and inched forward. The rafters groaned in protest and the heifer bellowed, but she was slowly lifted into the air. Though she jerked and wiggled the front part of her body, her back legs were still stiff and unmoving.

"It worked," Sky shouted over the roar of the tractor.

He killed the motor and jumped down. "Hot damn. That seemed too easy."

Sky bent under the rope and opened the gate to the stall. "She's trembling."

Coop followed her. "She's just weak and scared. Some feed and water will calm her down."

The cow had a good appetite, but Sky's eyes were once again drawn to her back legs, which showed no sign of movement. Did this animal have a chance, or were they wasting valuable time?

She rubbed the legs. "She has no feeling at all, does she?"

"No. But it could come back."

"It's a gamble, though?"

"Yep. Like most things in life."

"How long do we give her?"

He checked the ropes. "About a month."

"If there's no improvement then…" Somehow Sky couldn't say the words. That made her a bad rancher. She had to be able to take the hard knocks. How did Cait and Maddie do this?

The mere thought put fire in her backbone. If they could do it, then so could she.

COOPER WATCHED HER all during breakfast. For the first time, she was admitting the heifer might not survive. This wasn't the same woman who'd insisted on riding a prized thoroughbred in the dark of night, totally drunk. This woman had matured.

She was very gentle with the kid, patiently answering a million questions. But there was something in her eyes he couldn't define when she looked at the child. Was that sadness? She smiled and laughed, but it was still evident.

"I'm going to Georgie's birthday party," the kid said to no one in particular. "Do you want to go, Coo?"

He looked up, surprised. "Uh…I have work to do."

"It's Saturday," Miss Dorie said, "and Maddie would love to have you."

"Thanks, but I have to keep a close eye on the heifer."

"I'll bring you a piece of cake." Kira bobbed her head.

"There's no need." Suddenly, he had a suffocating feeling in his chest. He was a loner, and this attention was not something he accepted easily.

"But you like cake."

"Kira," her mother interjected. "It's time to get dressed. I promised Aunt Maddie I'd help today."

"'Kay." The kid slipped from the chair.

The redhead looked at him, her blue eyes warm and concerned. "Why don't you take the day off?"

He rose to his feet, avoiding eye contact. Looking into her eyes made him a little crazy, and he might find himself going to a birthday party. "Wouldn't know what to do with myself. I'll see y'all later."

"Bye, Coo," Kira called. She ran for the door, but slipped and fell. Loud wails filled the room.

Red picked her up and cuddled her. "Mommy's here."

"I fall down."

"I know." Red kissed her cheek. "I'll carry you upstairs."

Cooper watched as if mesmerized. Again, he thought, this wasn't the same girl he used to know. This woman cared. This was Dane Belle's daughter.

He couldn't figure out that look in her eyes, though. There was sadness, but there was also…worry?

What was the redhead worried about?

Was there something wrong with the kid?

Above the wails, Sky said, "I'll be back to help with the heifer."

"Don't worry about it. I'll let her down in a couple of hours and lift her again this afternoon." He reached for his hat. "I'm going to check on the hayfields to see how wet they are, and make sure those wild hogs haven't located the cornfield."

Cradling her child, she said, "You shouldn't work all day."

He didn't have a response for that. Work was his life, but Red actually seemed like she cared—about him. He could be dreaming. Or wishing?

Then he did something totally out of character. "Kira." He didn't know what made him call the child. Maybe it was her cries. The sound resonated with him. He'd had a lot to cry about as a kid.

Kira rubbed her eyes and peeped at him.

"Tell Georgie happy birthday for me."

"'Kay."

Then he made the mistake of looking at Red. Her eyes were soft and glowing like a blue flame. He felt a sucker punch to his chest.

"Have fun at the party," he said, and backed out of the room. Turning at the door, he bolted for freedom.

Sky watched him leave with a sinking feeling. He shouldn't work all the time. Everyone needed a day off. She would talk to Cait and Maddie about this.

Dressing Kira was becoming more difficult. She had her own opinions and most of the time they clashed with Sky's. The blue shorts with the gingham trim, matching top and sandals worked fine. Then Kira plopped the old hat on her head. A faded purple, it sported equally faded red feathers and yellow and green satin ribbons. The thing was atrocious and Sky couldn't imagine anyone wearing it, not even in the forties.

"Kira, baby, that's for play."

Gran swept into the room in an floppy old brown hat

with washed-out orange satin ribbons and a white feather. Sky swallowed all her protests.

"My babies, are you ready?"

"I'm ready." Kira ran to her.

"Then we must go. We do not keep people waiting."

Kira leaned against Gran with an impish grin. "Don't we look pretty, Mommy?"

"Absolutely," Sky replied, not bothering to hide a smile.

"We're…" Kira looked up at Gran. "Who are we?"

Gran straightened to her full height, her dignity intact. "Southern Belles, of course. But today we're Ingrid Bergman and Shirley Temple."

Kira nodded her head. "Yeah. That's who we are."

Just for fun, Sky said, "Shirley Temple didn't have red hair. It was more blond."

"Oh, Gran." Kira stomped her foot. "I can't be her. I got red hair."

"My baby," Gran replied calmly, "this is make-believe. You can have any color hair you want."

"I can still be her, then?"

"Yes, ma'am." Gran's eyes twinkled as she looked at Sky. "And we'll make your mom the Wicked Witch of the West."

Kira giggled, and so did Sky.

It was that kind of day—a fun day with family.

THE SUN WAS GOING DOWN when they returned to High Five. Georgie had a wonderful party and Maddie had outdone herself with the decorations. Kira enjoyed every moment, chasing and playing with Georgie and two other little boys who were in his play group. Watching her daughter, Sky thought there wasn't one sign anything was wrong with her.

But there was.

She could never forget that.

Gran went into the parlor to rest, and Sky thought she'd check on the heifer. Her daughter had other plans.

"Mommy, we have to take Coo his cake." Even with all the fun, Kira hadn't forgotten Cooper's cake. Sky knew she wouldn't, but didn't plan on taking it to him tonight. It could wait until morning.

"I don't know where Cooper is. We'll put it in the refrigerator for—"

"No. We have to do it now."

Sky looked down at her child. She was still wearing the purple hat, her blue eyes very determined. Sky had seen that look many times.

"Why?"

"Because I promised, and Gran said to never break a promise. It makes all the luck run out or something."

"That's when you hang a horseshoe upside down."

"It's the same thing, and Gran says you gotta have luck on your side."

Sky shook her head. Gran and her sayings were as outdated as the hat Kira was wearing. As she saw it, she had two choices: either make Kira go to bed, or give in. But she, too, wanted to see Cooper, to thank him for taking care of the heifer. At least that's what she told herself as she picked up her child and the cake and headed for the bunkhouse.

On the way they stopped to look in on the heifer. She was lying on the hay eating and didn't seem agitated.

"Cow got boo-boo, Mommy?"

"Yes." The stall was beginning to smell so Sky knew she'd have to clean it out tomorrow. Oh, God, what had she gotten herself into?

As she walked out of the barn, night had settled in like a lazy cat, stretching over the landscape. The moon provided enough light to see where she was going. Kira held tight to the cake.

When they rounded the corner of the barn, the bunkhouse came into view. The porch light was on and Cooper sat on the stoop, the dogs snoozing behind him.

"There's Coo, Mommy." Kira pointed.

"I see." She had no idea how he was going to feel about this visit, but they'd make it brief.

Cooper got to his feet as they neared the steps.

"Good evening," she said, looking up at him.

"We brought you cake." Kira could hardly contain her excitement.

Sky walked up the steps so Kira could give it to him. That close, she noticed he'd just taken a shower. His damp hair curled into his T-shirt, and a soapy clean scent reached her. He wore only the shirt and faded jeans, no shoes. In the porch light she could see his surprise.

Kira handed him the cake. "It's good. Aunt Maddie made it, and she put a fork in there, too."

"Thank you." He hesitated, then resumed his seat on the stoop.

Sky eased down by him with Kira on her lap. "I'm sorry if we're intruding, but she insisted we bring it tonight."

"'Cause our luck would run out," Kira told him.

He frowned.

"Don't ask," Sky said with a smile. Kira didn't give her time to say anything else.

"Look at my hat, Coo."

"Very pretty."

"I'm a temple."

He frowned again.

"She's supposed to be Shirley Temple. Gran was Ingrid Bergman."

He removed the plastic cover from the cake. "Miss Dorie playing make-believe again?"

"Yes, but this time it's not out of grief. It's for fun."

He took a bite. "She's a classy lady."

"Oh! Oh!" Kira spotted the dogs and got to her feet. "Coo got doggies."

"They're cow dogs."

Kira made a face. "I don't know what that means."

Coop finished the cake and set the paper plate aside. The dogs immediately trotted over to lick the crumbs. Kira's eyes opened wide.

"The one with the white feet is Boots. The one with the white on his neck is Bo. The other one's Booger. He's the youngest and gets into everything. If I have a sock or boot missing, I know who has it."

"Booger," Kira shouted.

"Yep."

"Can I play with them?"

He hesitated again. To a rancher a cow dog was a work dog and not a pet to be spoiled. Sky had heard that over the years from her father about the various dogs on the ranch. It hadn't stopped her, Cait or Maddie from playing with them.

"For Shirley Temple, sure."

"Oh, boy." Kira stepped onto the porch and the dogs gathered around her. She held out her hand and Boots licked it, then Booger sniffed her toes, while Bo licked her face. "They like me." Kneeling, she petted each one, her expression happy.

"Thank you," Sky said to Coop. "She loves animals."

They watched Kira and the dogs for a moment, then Sky asked, "How did your day go?"

"Fine. The hayfields are drying out and flourishing. We should be able to start cutting by next week."

"You didn't work all day, did you?"

"Nah. I quit early. Saturday is my laundry day."

She scrunched up her face. "How boring."

"That's my life and I like it that way. I'm tired of stares and pointed fingers. I'm content right here."

She'd asked Cait and Maddie about Cooper's time off. They said he never took any. They'd tried talking to him about it, but he always resisted, so they left him in peace. She might find that hard to do.

"So how was the party?"

The quick change of subject didn't escape her. "Great. Maddie made everything, from the cake to all the decorations, which included tiny Curious Georges as gifts. Little Georgie loved that."

"Maddie puts her heart into everything."

"That's my sister. I'm so glad Kira had her birthday in early May or she'd be expecting me to do all that crafty stuff. Maddie made a Curious George cake from scratch. I've never made a cake in my life."

"It can't be that hard. You can buy a cake mix and I believe you can buy the icing, too."

"How do you know that?"

"I used to work for a lady who made cakes all the time."

"Was she trying to get your attention?" The words were out before Sky could snatch them back.

Instead of getting angry, he quirked his lips. "No, she was almost seventy and very nice."

Sky's mouth curved slightly. "Unlike Everett."

That didn't make him angry, either. "Everett was a wheeler-dealer and he liked the ladies."

"I know. My mother was his third wife."

He rested his elbows on his knees and clasped his hands between his legs. "What happened to your mom?"

"When Everett's money was gone, so was my mother."

Coop looked at her, startled, but didn't say anything.

"I don't wear rose-colored glasses when it comes to my mother. I love her, but at times I've found it hard to like her."

"That's very candid."

The wind blew a strand of hair across her face and she brushed it back. "That's the only way I can be. I spent years rebelling, wanting my mother to be someone she wasn't. She's not a stay-at-home, one-man type of woman, but she believes in love and keeps searching for Mr. Right." Sky paused and ran her fingers down the thighs of her jeans. "When you were at the Rocking C, did you ever meet her?"

"Only from a distance. Her opinion of the cowboys was much the same as yours."

"Hey." Sky slapped his arm playfully. "I apologized for that, and I've changed a lot since Kira was born."

"Yes. I think you have."

"Thank you very much." Her eyes caught his. "Having total responsibility for her has been an eye-opening, scary experience. I'm so afraid I'm doing something wrong."

"You don't seem to be." He clasped his hands tighter. "Where's her father?"

Sky stared out into the darkness and a peaceful quiet settled around them. Telling her story wasn't easy, and she didn't do it often. There was too much at stake. But talking to Cooper seemed natural. Comfortable.

"I met Todd Spencer at one of the many parties I used

to attend. He was rich, handsome and educated. We always had fun together—that was my number-one goal in life at the time. He lives off a family trust fund and we jetted all over the country, partying and gambling. That was during my insane years, as I like to call them."

She took a long breath. "Another goal was to never be like my mother, with a string of husbands, so Todd and I moved in together. My dad didn't like it, and went so far as to say Todd wasn't the man for me and I needed to grow up. He was right. The moment Todd found out I was pregnant he told me I was on my own. He didn't want kids. He packed his bags and left. I haven't seen him since."

Coop's eyes narrowed. "Does he call about the kid?"

"No. He has no interest in Kira, but his parents do."

She told him about the Spencers and their quest to take Kira from her.

"I've heard it's hard to take a child from the mother."

"Not when they have high-priced attorneys and the mother's past isn't perfect." She glanced at him. "You could even testify against me."

His eyes darkened. "I would never do that."

"But there are a lot of people who knew me when I was out of control, and some of those good ol' sorority sisters would probably stick a knife in my back without a second thought. I'm now one of the poor people and not in their crowd anymore."

He stared at her for a moment and then said, "I'm sorry I was rude to you. I'm sorry I misjudged you."

Her breath caught in her throat at the look in his eyes. He was sincere, open and… A wispy snore interrupted her thoughts.

"Oh, my." She jumped to her feet. Kira was sound

asleep on Boots, the purple hat cockeyed. "Oh, my baby." She scooped her up and kissed her cheek. "She's worn-out from the big day. It's definitely past her bedtime."

Cooper got to his feet, watching Sky with her little girl. He didn't see how anyone could take the child from her, it was so clear how much she loved her. Maybe that's what he'd seen in her eyes, the sadness and worry.

All his protective instincts kicked in…but why? She didn't need his protection. She didn't need him, period.

He picked up the hat and handed it to her. "Thanks for the cake."

"My daughter wouldn't have it any other way. Sorry I talked your ear off."

"They say talk is good, but I've never been a big fan of it. In this case, though, it *was* good. I saw you so differently."

"Uh, yeah. The bitch."

"Yeah." He nodded with a grin.

She went down the steps and stopped at the bottom, the light shimmering on her red hair. He'd never seen hair quite that color. It wasn't carrot or auburn, but somewhere in between. It reminded him of the rich color of leaves in the fall.

"Thanks for taking care of the heifer. She looks so much better."

"Vitamins and antibiotics have perked her up."

Kira moved against her and moaned. "'Night. I have to get her to bed."

"'Night, Red."

A smile split her face. "As a kid, I used to smack people for calling me that. But at the moment I have my hands full. I'll get you, though."

He watched as she walked off into the darkness. Picking up the paper plate from the step, he grinned. Getting slapped by her could be the highlight of his life.

He had to be on guard, however. Skylar Belle was his boss and way out of his league.

CHAPTER SEVEN

THE NEXT MORNING Cooper gave the heifer another round of shots. When he lifted her she struggled to move—a good sign. As long as she had a will to fight, she just might make it.

He jumped off the tractor and paused as he saw the little girl standing in the barn doorway. She wore a lavender gown with lace around the neck and hem, no shoes, and her stuffed animal was clutched in one arm. Red curls poked out in all directions. Obviously, she'd just woken up. Where was the redhead?

"Hi," Kira said, yawning. "Can I play with your dogs?"

He walked to her. "Where's your mother?"

"Kira! Kira! Kira!" The frantic cries vibrated though the old barn.

"Uh-oh." Kira made a face.

"She's in here," Cooper called.

Red rushed in, out of breath. She glanced at her daughter and then at him. "What's she doing here?"

"I looked up and there she was."

He had a hard time glancing away from the redhead in a sleeveless nightshirt and nothing else. Her feet were bare, as were her long, smooth legs. Her hair stuck out just like her daughter's, but to him it looked sexy and dreamy, probably the way she looked after...

Squatting in front of Kira, she said, "You are not to leave the house without permission."

"I saw the doggies out the window and I wanted to play with them."

Sky shook a finger in the girl's face. "Not without permission."

Kira stuck out her lower lip and Sky swung her into her arms.

"I want to play with the doggies."

"No. You disobeyed and you're going to the house for a time-out."

"No! No! No!" Kira screamed, trying to wiggle down.

Sky pointed a finger at Kira's face and shook it again. "Stop it, Kira Dane Belle, this instant."

Kira laid her head on her mom's shoulder, sobbing, and the two made their way to the house.

The dogs sat on their haunches, staring after them, but made no move to follow. "Scared, huh?"

All three stood and whined.

The redhead was frightened out of her mind, and Coop could only surmise that it had something to do with the ex-boyfriend's parents.

Her fear became very real to him, though.

NEITHER RED NOR THE KID were at breakfast, so Coop knew discipline was being enforced.

Skully and his boys arrived, and Rufus was talking to them when Sky came out of the house. Ru introduced her. Coop stood by the barn, but made no move to join the conversation.

Skully was a small man with an even smaller brain. He resembled a weasel and was just as sneaky.

"I'll trap your hogs, ma'am, but I don't work with Cooper Yates."

Coop tensed and wanted to disappear, but he stood his ground. He would never bow to a man like Skully.

"Then take your small mind and get off my property," Sky replied.

"Those hogs can do a lot of damage."

"And so can idiots like you." She walked off and left Skully standing with his mouth gaping open.

The redhead walked right past Coop and into the barn. She bent low under the rope and went into the heifer's stall. Stroking and talking soothingly, she massaged the cow's back legs.

Leaning on the gate, he said, "You didn't have to do that."

"Yes, I did." She didn't look up, just kept working.

"I'm used to the attitudes of the townsfolk."

"You shouldn't be."

"I don't need you to fight my battles." His tone wasn't rough. He was just stating his opinion.

She walked out of the stall and sat on a bale of hay. "Don't you get angry?"

"All the time, but I've learned that anger leads to destructive behavior."

She tucked a loose strand of hair behind her ear. "You're talking about the beating you gave Everett."

"Yeah." He sat beside her. "If I had just walked away, I'd be a free man today, untarnished by my actions."

"You can't walk away forever."

"I think you're trying too hard."

Sky snapped her head around. "What are you talking about?"

Meeting her gaze, he replied, "We got off to a rocky

start and you're trying to make amends by defending me."

She opened her mouth and then closed it. "Maybe. With my past, I have no right to judge anyone."

"Neither do I."

She laughed and he liked the sound—tingly, musical and soothing. "We're a pair, aren't we?"

He stood. "Yeah. Let's stop trying so hard and just be ourselves."

"That would leave you working yourself to death and hiding away in the bunkhouse."

"That's my choice."

"Mmm." She kicked at the dirt with her boot.

"Where's the kid?"

"Time-out in her room, but I know she's peeping out the door, trying to tempt Gran and Etta."

"It's none of my business, but didn't you overreact a little?"

"Maybe, but I have this fear of losing her." She took a breath. "When I couldn't find her, I just lost it."

"You think your boyfriend's parents will sneak in and steal her?"

"I'm not sure what they'll do. I have to be on guard at all times."

"You need a lawyer."

"That takes money."

"One way or another, you have to fight this and stop being afraid."

She lifted an eyebrow. "Wasn't I just telling you the same thing?"

"Not the same— Damn it…" He switched gears as Solomon moseyed into the barn. "That bull doesn't know what a pen is for."

"As long as we keep the gate closed, he can't hurt the heifer." Sky got to her feet. "I better check on my kid. Oh. I promised her after time-out we'd go on a picnic with the dogs."

"Sure. They'll follow you anywhere, especially if you have food."

Her eyes caught his. "You're going, too."

"Oh, no. I've got things to do." No way was he getting involved in a picnic. He didn't do the family thing.

"It's Sunday. You're taking the afternoon off."

He frowned. "Didn't we just have this discussion of being ourselves? Well, I, for one, do not do picnics."

"Tell that to Kira, then."

He shook his head. "That's your job."

Red placed her hands on her hips. "You really are a recluse, and a stubborn ass to boot."

"Yep, and don't forget it." He grabbed Solomon's halter and led the bull into the corral. When he turned around, the redhead was gone.

And that suited him fine.

WHEN SKY WALKED INTO the parlor, Gran stopped pacing and turned to her. "Is it time to let Kira out?"

"She's not in prison."

"I don't like you disciplining her. She cried for a long time."

"I don't like it, either, but she's too little to leave the house on her own. What if Cooper or Rufus were backing out a tractor and didn't see her? She's so small anything could happen. I want her to mind."

"Well, her mother never did," Gran retorted in a voice Sky rarely heard.

"Exactly. I don't want her to be impulsive, daring, and always breaking the rules."

Gran lifted an eyebrow. "And making a few of her own."

Sky grimaced. "I wasn't that bad, was I?"

"I didn't meet my great-granddaughter until she was three years old."

"Oh, Gran." Sky hugged her. "I'm sorry I'm such an awful granddaughter."

Gran drew back. "You're not awful. You're Dane's spirited daughter and the light of my life. But neither Dane nor I understood some of your choices. We always thought you were trying to prove something. We just never knew what that was."

Sky took a long breath and admitted something for the first time. "Maybe that I could be as strong as Cait and as sweet as Maddie."

"But you're Sky. You're a fighter, a survivor—a true Belle."

"So are Cait and Maddie."

"Ah, but Skylar does it the hard way—her way."

"I love you, Gran." They embraced again. Even though Gran could make her feel guilty, she could also make her feel good about herself.

"Cait's picking me up for the day. May I please see Kira before I leave?"

"Yes, ma'am. I will get her."

When she opened the bedroom door, she saw Kira curled up on the bed, still in her nightgown. Sky's heart twisted. Being a mother was hell sometimes.

She eased onto the bed and Kira sat up.

"I'm being good, Mommy." Her blue eyes were red from crying.

Sky pulled her into her arms and held her tightly. "Precious, do you understand what you did wrong?"

"I went to play with the doggies," Kira muttered.

"That's part of it, but what's the real reason?"

Kira looked up at her and shrugged.

"Think."

"I'm not supposed to play with the doggies."

"No. That's not it."

Kira stared blankly.

"What did Mommy tell you?"

Kira shrugged.

"You can't leave the house without permission. Permission, Kira."

"Oh."

"Do you understand what I'm saying?"

She nodded. "Mommy?"

"What?"

"What's permission?"

Sky sighed. "You can't leave the house without asking Mommy. You can't go anywhere alone. Now do you understand?"

"Uh-huh."

"Good." She squeezed her child. "Now go downstairs and tell Gran bye. She's going to Aunt Cait's."

Kira scooted off the bed. "And we're going on a picnic, Mommy?"

"Yes."

"With the doggies?"

"Yes."

"Oh, boy." Kira darted out of the room.

Sky sagged against the pillow, thinking a picnic with the dogs was more of a reward instead of a punishment. She was never going to get mothering right. But she was trying.

She walked over to the window and saw Cooper galloping away on the paint. Away from them. He wasn't sticking around for a picnic.

Cait and Maddie had said that he was a loner and rarely left the ranch. She wondered if he was punishing himself and didn't even realize it. Or did he just not want to spend any time with her?

Be ourselves.

She drew a long breath and decided to stop feeling guilty and just enjoy the afternoon with her daughter.

THE HAYFIELDS WERE DRYING out fast. In a few days Cooper knew he'd be able to start cutting. The corn was thriving, too, and he had to watch it closely. Now that Red had gotten rid of Skully the wild hogs would be a threat.

He didn't need her to champion his cause. He just needed her to make sound decisions on running High Five. His battles were his own and no one else's.

And he didn't want her involving him in family affairs. He was the hired hand, and that's how he wanted it to stay. It might sound strange to her, but he was happier that way.

In the late afternoon he checked the herd, then crossed Crooked Creek, heading for the bunkhouse. He heard laughter and turned Rebel toward the sound.

Red sat on a blanket under a huge oak tree, its branches fanning out over the water. The kid was throwing a stick, and the dogs raced each other to get to it first, so they could bring it back to her.

Childish giggles mingled with the wind on the warm afternoon. It was infectious and...

Keep going. Keep moving. This wasn't his scene.

Against every sane thought in his head, he guided Rebel toward them, intending only to say hi.

The kid saw him and came running, shouting, "Coo! Coo!"

In a straw hat and sunglasses, Red turned in his direction. Her arms were bare in the tank top, and tight jeans molded her hips and legs. He found he was staring.

"Coo," Kira kept chanting, and his gaze swung to her. "We're playing." The dogs wagged their tails and lapped up the attention like gravy. "Play with us."

"I have—"

"Please." Those baby-blue eyes were hard to resist, and the next thing he knew, he was dismounting.

"Watch me," Kira called, then was off running, the dogs at her heels.

He eased down on the blanket and leaned against the oak. Red didn't say a word and neither did he. It was peaceful and quiet here on the creek. Blackbirds landed in a tree and a squirrel scurried across the grass.

Removing his hat, Coop placed it on the blanket. Kira ran toward them, tripped and fell. Loud sobs echoed through the woods. Red was immediately on her feet, as was he.

Red picked up the child and carried her back to the blanket, offering soothing words. "You're okay. Mommy's here."

"I hurt my knee, Mommy," Kira sobbed.

Cooper noticed that her right knee was red and swollen. She'd fallen more on her stomach than her knee, so she must have twisted it. The dogs whined, obviously anxious.

Red opened the picnic basket, pulled out a bottle of liquid Tylenol and gave the girl a dose. She kissed her. "Now it will stop hurting, my precious."

So many memories pounded at Cooper—memories of his mother. No one had been that loving or caring to him since. He treasured those times, of a boy and his mother. But they seemed to belong to someone else. He'd almost forgotten about those rare moments in his life.

"Look, the dogs are waiting," Red said.

"I'm fine." Kira rubbed her tear-filled eyes. "I'm gonna play now." She stood and limped to the dogs.

"Is she okay?" Cooper asked.

"No, but I have to pretend that she is." Red removed her sunglasses and wiped away a tear. Coop felt a catch in his throat.

"What do you mean?"

"Hasn't Rufus told you?"

"No."

"Kira has juvenile arthritis."

"What?"

"It's in the early stages, and so far it's not the serious kind. But as she grows that could change. She could go into remission or she might be dealing with it for the rest of her life."

"I had no idea."

"Another reason I have to keep my child. She needs me, and I will never let the Spencers take her."

"It's time to talk to an attorney." Coop didn't know why he was offering advice; that's wasn't his style. But the thought of Red being separated from Kira was unbearable.

"Would you go with me?" As soon as the words left her mouth, she backpedaled. "Never mind. I don't know why I asked that. I have my sisters and Gran."

"You don't need an ex-con on your side."

She slapped his arm. "Don't say that. You didn't do anything that any normal person wouldn't do."

"Tell that to the folks of High Cotton."

"My sisters learned a long time ago never to say things like that because I'd do it."

"That I can picture." His gaze centered on Kira, sitting on the edge of the blanket, the dogs' heads resting in her lap.

"Kira likes you unconditionally," Red added. "That speaks for itself."

"You're so good with her. Reminds me of my mother." Did he say that out loud?

Red sat cross-legged, facing him. "Is she still living?"

He had, and now he had to respond. He swallowed. "She died unexpectedly from a brain tumor when I was eight." That was all the sharing he was prepared to do.

"That had to have been difficult for a small boy."

"Yeah." He drew up his knees and rested his forearms on them, his hands clasped tight. "She was the buffer between my dad and me." Against his will the words kept coming. "He was an abusive, horrible man. After my mother died, it got worse. I spent most of my childhood hiding from him, but eventually he'd find me and he'd beat me with a belt. I still have scars on my back."

Her hand touched his forearm. "Why didn't someone do something?"

"CPS took me away twice, but sent me back both times. When I reached sixteen, I was a pretty good size. One night I yanked the belt away from him and he knew I was big enough to protect myself. He never hit me after that, just cussed at me. I was glad to leave High Cotton and him behind."

Her hand tightened and he glanced down at her fingers. "What happened to him?" she murmured.

"He died a year after I left. His truck stalled on a railroad track and a train was coming. Instead of getting out, he kept trying to start the engine. The train hit him full force."

Coop kept staring at her perfectly shaped fingers. "I vowed I would never be like him, but I beat Everett just like my dad beat me—without mercy. You can try, but you can't outrun your genes."

Kira's head bobbed and he jumped up to catch her before she fell over, asleep. He cradled her in his arms and had a hard time catching his breath.

"Coo," she murmured sleepily.

Sky got to her feet, her eyes on Cooper. Anyone that gentle with a child could never hurt anyone. "I'll take her. Tylenol always makes her sleepy."

"It's okay. I got her." He seemed not to want to let her go.

"We better get back so I can get her to bed."

Sky gathered their things and packed them on her horse, Blaze. Turning, she saw that Cooper had mounted with Kira in his arms. Slowly they made their way to the barn, the dogs following.

She took Kira from him then, her hands brushing his taut muscles as an outdoorsy scent drifted to her.

"I'll take care of the horses," he said. "And look in on the heifer."

Her eyes caught his. "You're nothing like your father."

"But he is my father and I can lose my temper at the drop of a hat."

To avoid that, he kept to himself, working until he

couldn't think or enjoy life. He was still in his own self-made prison.

Cradling Kira in one arm, Sky stood on tiptoe and reached up with one hand to clasp his neck. He tensed, but it didn't stop her. She stroked his roughened skin and felt the texture of his thick hair curling into his collar.

His eyes darkened, and she pulled him toward her, meeting the firm line of his lips gently, softly. One touch and emotions exploded within them. He cupped her face and took over the kiss with a deep, yearning intensity.

He tasted of sunshine and the outdoors. As he caressed her lips, a sensual heat built in her and mingled with the wildness in both of them. His callused hands held her face, but all she felt was his power—in her and all around her. A gentle power that was riveting. Evocative. Real.

The kiss went on and on, bonding them together in a new way—as a man and a woman.

He broke the kiss and breathed in deeply. "Red—"

"That was without trying," she interrupted. "Think about it." Saying that, she walked out of the barn on shaky legs.

CHAPTER EIGHT

KIRA WOKE UP several times during the night, crying, so Sky didn't get much sleep. She was late for breakfast, and Coop and Rufus had already gone. Rufus came in for lunch, but Cooper didn't. Ru said the hogs had rooted up part of the cornfield and Cooper was making sure they kept away.

Guilt nudged her conscience, but she wasn't giving in to Skully Lutz and his kind. While Kira was in the parlor with Gran, Sky did paperwork and made phone calls. Judd gave her a couple of hog hunters' names and thirty minutes later she hired Otis Greensage. She asked if he had a problem with Cooper Yates and he said he didn't know who the man was. That was even better. She told Otis she wanted him on the property today. Cooper had too much to do to worry about the hogs.

Otis arrived at two o'clock, pulling a long cattle trailer with three horses inside. Four hunting dogs rode in the bed of his Dodge truck. His two brothers, Delmar and Remus, were also with him. Otis was a big black man with a hearty laugh and a jovial attitude. Sky liked him instantly.

"Now, Ms. Belle." He rested his hands on his ample hips, his dark eyes direct and honest. "You do realize we might have to shoot some of these hogs."

"Yes, but only as a last resort."

He tipped his hat. "You got it."

Cooper galloped into the barn just then. "That's my foreman, Cooper Yates. He'll take you to the place he saw the hogs."

Otis followed her to the barn and she introduced the two men. Cooper glanced at her with that surprised look she was becoming accustomed to. She left them to discuss the situation.

Sky spent the rest of the afternoon cleaning out the heifer's stall. It was a dirty, thankless job, but after every muscle and bone in her body was aching, the cow had a clean, fresh place to get well.

After letting her down with the tractor, she fed her and headed for the house and a bath.

She kept an eye out for Otis and his crew, but as dusk fell he still wasn't back. And neither was Cooper. Sky put Kira down for the night and waited.

It was after eight when she heard the clang of the trailer. Otis stopped when he saw her in the yard. In the front of the trailer were two mama pigs, a large boar and about ten baby pigs.

"Had a good day, Ms. Belle."

"I see."

"Cooper was a big help. We caught the mamas and the babies in the traps. That big boar was a problem, but Cooper roped him and my dogs took him down. If you have any more problems, call me."

"Thank you."

The trailer clanged out of sight.

Cooper hadn't had supper and she knew he wouldn't come to the house this late. She fixed a plate of smothered steak, mashed potatoes, green beans and a roll.

"Gran," she called, hurrying into the parlor. "Would you listen for Kira, please? I'm carrying Cooper his supper."

"Really." Gran turned from the TV set.

"Yes, and if I don't return, don't come looking for me." She winked.

"Skylar Dane Belle."

"Gran, I'm joking."

"I know, but I love the way your face matches your hair."

"It does not. I stopped blushing when I was about eighteen."

"If you say so." Gran got to her feet with a smile. "I'll go up so I can hear my baby."

"Thank you. I won't be long." Sky paused at the door. "Really."

Gran winked, then went up the stairs.

Good grief, her grandmother could read her like a very naughty book.

As Sky walked through the moonlit night, she wondered why she was making this effort. She had said that she wouldn't, but she and Coop had come a long way since then. They knew each other better, and everything she knew she liked. But most of all she didn't want Cooper to spend the rest of his life in a self-made prison. Any part she could play in changing that she would embrace wholeheartedly.

A bright yellow moon hung in the sky. The sight made her smile. When she was six, she had wandered away from her mother, who'd been trying on clothes in a mall. It took two hours before the police had found her sitting on the floor in a toy store, lost and afraid. After that, Sky became fearful of the dark and didn't want to sleep by herself. Probably the only time in her life she'd been afraid of anything.

Julia didn't know how to deal with her, so that year she'd sent Sky early to Texas for the summer. Her father had sat with her on the veranda and pointed to the moon. He'd said that God was a big and powerful presence and the moon was a gold medallion he wore around his neck. So when she saw the yellow light she knew that God was right there watching over her.

It worked for a six-year-old, and ironically, at times it still worked for the thirty-one-year old Skylar, especially when it came to Kira.

Actually, she might need a little of its power tonight.

COOPER TOOK A SHOWER and pulled on clean, faded jeans. He grabbed a cold beer out of the refrigerator and walked out to the front porch. The dogs sniffed his bare feet.

Sitting on the stoop, he petted them, and they got comfortable by his side. He took a swig from the bottle and enjoyed the quiet of the evening. After he relaxed from the long day, he'd fix a sandwich or something. He was more tired than hungry, though.

He sensed her before she came into view. The warm air was suddenly charged with electricity as Sky sashayed to within a few feet of him. Her red hair was loose and curled around her face. Her skin was bare and those fetching freckles were visible across her nose. In a white sleeveless top and blue jeans, she looked fresh and inviting.

She plunked down beside him and handed him a plate. "I brought your supper."

Taking the dish, he said, "I thought you weren't going to do that anymore."

"It's a special occasion."

"What would that be?"

She clapped her hands. "You caught the hogs."

He set the plate between them. "Where did you find Otis?"

She cocked her head. "I'm very resourceful."

"Yeah, and thanks. Now I can concentrate on the hay. Think I'll start cutting in a couple of days. It'll be a steady pace well into July."

"The ranch is doing better. Much better. I spoke with Mr. Bardwell this morning and he's going to start hauling sand and gravel again. That will be more revenue."

Coop glanced off into the darkness. "It's been a year now and High Five is back on track. If we get through the summer and don't have any catastrophes like the hurricane, then the ranch will be back in business."

"Thanks to you."

His heart skipped a beat at her praise. "Thanks to the Belle sisters, who stuck it out."

"Cait didn't give us much of a choice, but we still have a long way to go."

A comfortable silence ensued as they listened to the crickets and the howl of a coyote.

"How's Kira?"

"She had a bad night, but she was running around playing today."

"I still can't believe someone so small has arthritis."

"It's a constant worry, but I find it helps to be home with family."

He didn't answer because he didn't know much about the family thing, but he knew the Belles would always be there for the redhead.

Silence intruded again and he reached for his beer on the stoop. "Would you like a beer?"

"No, thanks. I have to get back." She turned to face him. "Since I haven't seen you all day I thought you might be avoiding me."

"Why?" He ran his thumb over the label of the cold beer.

"Because I kissed you."

His hand tightened on the bottle. "I've been kissed before."

"Mmm. By how many women?"

He quirked an eyebrow at her. "I didn't keep count."

"Pity. It would make for an interesting conversation."

"Not by me."

"Not a talker, huh?"

"Nope."

"I kissed you because I wanted to. You said we should be ourselves, and that's me—very impulsive. I take what I want."

"I don't think you're that person anymore."

"Maybe. But there's chemistry between us. It's been there from the start."

They were getting in too deep and he had to back off. There was no future in encouraging Red. But it felt good sitting in the moonlight with her.

"I can feel you shutting down," she said, to his surprise.

"I'm being realistic."

"I'm being optimistic." She reached over and kissed his cheek, and didn't move away. Her breath fanned his skin and a sweet, seductive scent reached him. Her lips traveled to his bare shoulder and her tongue licked and tasted. Every muscle in his body tensed and he had a hard time controlling his breathing and other reactions.

"Red…"

She wasn't listening as her lips traveled to his back.

They stopped at his scarred skin. He froze. Then she ran her tongue along one welt. Liquid fire shot through him.

"Please stop," he choked out.

"Don't you feel the chemistry?" she whispered.

"I feel a lot of things, but what I feel most is that we have to stop."

"Why?"

"Trust me, we do."

She rose to her feet and suddenly he felt bereft. Flipping back her hair, she said, "I'll let you get away with that tonight, but someday soon we'll discuss it again."

"I don't think so."

"Your past doesn't bother me."

"It did once." He sounded like a petulant child, instead of a man starving for her touch.

They stared at each other, and there it was, as bright as the moon—his past. It stood between them and always would.

"Let it go, Cooper." The words were almost a plea, which he had to ignore.

Reaching for the plate, he stood. "Thanks for the food."

She swung around and disappeared into the darkness.

He let out a long breath and went inside. As tempting as Red was, he couldn't let her get to him.

But how did he forget her touch?

Or that look in her blue eyes?

TODD SPENCER STRODE through his parents' front door with a purpose—to get the two of them out of his life.

He found them in the sunroom, eating breakfast. His mother was immaculate in a silk peignoir and his father wore his usual Ralph Lauren pajamas and robe. His face was buried in a newspaper.

"I want you to stop interfering in my life." Todd's loud words bounced off the walls.

"Oh, my darling." His mother feigned surprise. "How wonderful to see you."

"Cut the crap and call off the P.I."

His father laid down the paper. "What are you talking about?"

"A man searched my condo in Palm Springs."

"How do you know it was a P.I.?"

"I live in an exclusive resort that requires an ID to get in. The man used my best friend Corey's address and info. There's only one place he could have gotten that and that's from you. What do you want?"

"Now, son…"

"What do you want?"

"After two years, a cordial hello would be nice," his mother said.

"Just tell me what the hell you're looking for."

His parents glanced at each other.

"Oh, God, it's about Skylar Belle again, isn't it?"

His mother shifted to face him. "Now that you brought her up…"

"There is no kid, Mother, so let it go."

"She's been seen with a child—a little girl," his father pointed out.

"So? She's not mine, and why the hell do you care about a grandchild? You never cared about your own son."

His mother rose to her feet. "You know why, Todd. If she's a Spencer…"

"She's not, so leave me and Skylar Belle the freakin' hell alone."

"I do not appreciate that language."

"Stuff it." He swung out of the room and, he hoped, out of their lives forever.

Cybil resumed her seat. "What do you think?"

"I think he's protesting too much."

She picked up her china cup. "When will the DNA test be ready?"

"Since the P.I. managed to find some of Todd's hair, he said it might be two weeks."

"Let's hope the test is negative and we can put this to rest once and for all."

MAY GAVE WAY TO JUNE and constant work. Sky didn't see much of Cooper. He was busy in the hayfields, and she took care of the heifer and the cattle. Since she had an up-close-and-personal relationship with the cow, she decided to name her Sassy. Her father always said naming the ranch animals was a no-no, but in this case she relented.

She usually took lunch to Cooper and Rufus. Kira wanted to go, too, so Sky let her. Gran needed a midday break. Sky bought a straw sun hat for Kira that tied under her chin. With June came a wave of heat and she didn't want her to get sunburned.

Kira was becoming more and more attached to Cooper, and he wasn't pushing her away, as he did Sky. Cooper was now Kira's number-one hero.

He had put latches on all the entry doors in the house, simple hooks and eyes high enough that Kira couldn't reach them. Sky was touched by his thoughtfulness.

Late one afternoon she took iced tea to the guys and Kira came along with the dogs. The last bale of hay had been harvested from that field and the men were quitting for the day. It was the first time in two weeks they'd quit before seven.

Coop drank a plastic glass of tea and wiped the sweat from his forehead. "We'll take the tractors back to the lean-to and grease them before we start in the morning on the next field."

"Coo." Kira bounced up and down at his feet, the straw hat wobbling. "Can I ride with you?"

"Cooper's going on the tractor," Sky explained.

He took one last swig from the glass and handed it to her. "It's okay. I'll take her. The sun's not so bad right now."

"Oh, boy. Oh, boy."

"Come on, sunshine." Cooper swung Kira into his arms and crawled onto the tractor. He placed her directly in front of him. The tractor puttered to life and they pulled away.

Sky didn't worry. She knew Cooper would take very good care of her daughter.

The dogs whined at her feet.

"It's just you and me, guys. Let's go." They jumped into the truck bed and they started home, with Rufus trailing in the rear.

Sky parked at the barn and Kira came running, her straw hat bobbing, her eyes bright.

"Did you see me, Mommy? Did you see me? I drove. Coo let me drive all by myself."

The dogs jumped to get her attention and Kira fell with them to the ground, giggling. It was great to see her child so happy.

Cooper came around the barn. "Down, boys. Down!" he shouted. The dogs rolled to attention, as did Kira, who had a confused look on her face.

"What's wrong?" Sky asked, a little puzzled at his stern voice.

"They might hurt her."

She lifted an eyebrow.

"They won't hurt me," Kira told him. "They love me."

"Sometimes they get a little exuberant."

Kira shook her head. "I don't know what that means."

"It means...go play."

Kira ran into the barn, but the dogs looked at Cooper. He flung out a hand. "Go." The dogs charged after her.

Sky kept her eyebrow lifted.

"Yes, I overreacted," he said.

"You think?"

"Let's put the heifer down before you give me a lecture."

"Her name is Sassy."

"What?"

"The heifer. That's her name."

"Oh, good Lord."

Sky linked her arm through his. He didn't pull away as she expected. "I've been cleaning her stall and massaging her legs for weeks, so I thought she deserved a name."

"You're too softhearted to be a rancher."

She poked him in the chest with her other hand. "Take that back."

Stopping, he looked into her eyes, and her knees felt weak from the warm glow she saw there. "But just softhearted enough for a woman."

Holding his gaze, she experienced the most sensual feeling she'd ever had. She didn't want to move or do anything but feel his eyes all over her.

"Mommy," Kira called, and then they heard a low, distressed bellow.

They hurried into the barn, then stood completely still when they reached the stall. Sassy was standing on all fours in the harness—a little wobbly, but she was standing.

"Oh my God, look." Sky couldn't believe her eyes. "She's better. She's going to make it."

Sky threw her arms around Cooper's neck and hugged him. He hugged her back and they gazed at each other. In that moment she knew that not only was Sassy better, but Cooper was, too.

He was opening his heart, little by little, and the guilt that kept him bound in solitude was slowly letting go.

She kissed him briefly. "We did it."

"Yes, we did."

CHAPTER NINE

LEO GARVEY, the P.I., laid the DNA results in front of the Spencers. "It's ninety-nine point nine. The child is definitely Todd Spencer's daughter."

"I will speak to my attorney," Jonathan said, fingering the report. "In the meantime, step up the investigation. Hire extra people if you have to. I want Skylar Belle and the child found."

"Yes, sir. I'm on it." The investigator left the room.

"Seems our son lied." Cybil reached for her glasses and studied the papers.

"He's always been good at that." Jonathan shifted uncomfortably in his chair. "Todd wants nothing to do with the child. I suppose we could just sweep this under the rug."

Cybil removed her glasses. "I don't think that's wise. This could come back to haunt us in the future. It's better to take care of it now."

"Yes. Yes, you're right. I'll contact Carl Devlin, so he can be ready to file for temporary custody as soon as the child is located."

BY THE END OF JUNE all the hay was baled and off the fields. Sky spent long days beside Cooper, working. She drove the tractor with the three-point forklift to cart the round bales to the fence for storage. She wore long-sleeved blouses and a floppy hat to protect her skin. By the end of the day her body was soaked in sweat, and she wondered if she was the same Skylar Belle who had never done a day's work in her life.

She knew she wasn't. Rebellion wasn't even in her character anymore. Her child and her home had become her top priorities. She used to scoff at Caitlyn and her passion for High Five, but now she understood it. The ranch was their legacy, inherited from their father, and like Cait, Sky would work her fingers to the bone to make sure Dane Belle's life's work would flourish.

Cooper hadn't said so, but she knew he had the same feelings for High Five. She marveled at his strength, his abilities and his energy. If a tractor broke, he fixed it. If the baler stopped working, he made it go again. There didn't seem to be anything he couldn't do. They even quit early one day to round up calves to haul to auction. His energy never stopped.

Sky knew he was still trying to outrun his demons. But High Five gave him the peace he needed.

After a long day, she leaned on the stall gate and watched Sassy take small steps. It was an absolute miracle. The heifer had been able to get to her feet on her own for a week.

Cooper walked up behind her, carrying Kira, who'd been playing with the dogs. "Soon we can put her in the corral."

"Do you think Solomon will hurt her?"

"Nah. They'll be fine. But I'd like for her to get a little stronger first."

"Me, too." Sky tickled her daughter's stomach. "You don't have legs when Cooper's around."

Kira giggled and raised her arms. "Coo lifts me high."

The dogs whined, and Kira wriggled down. "Gotta go play." She ran into the corral, the dogs chasing her.

"Kira," Sky called, worried the dogs might spook Solomon.

As if reading her mind, Coop said, "Don't worry. Solomon is in his pen for a change."

She reached up and wiped the sweat from his forehead, her fingers lingering for a moment on his warm skin.

"Damn, it's hot," he said, removing his hat and finishing the job with the sleeve of his chambray shirt. "I need a shower."

"Wanna take one together?" She winked with a sly grin.

He leaned in, his green eyes twinkling, and whispered, "What would you do if I said yes?"

"Ask and find out."

He rocked back on his heels. "You're a big tease."

"Maybe." She poked him in the chest. "But I'm serious about *this*. Kira and I would be honored if you'd take us to the Fourth of July barbecue at the Southern Cross Ranch."

He groaned. "Red, I don't do the social thing."

"I know." She smoothed the fabric of his shirt across his chest, taking her time over those rock-hard muscles. "It's time to stop hiding and face these people." She stepped closer. "Please…for me."

Kira came running, and Sky said a silent prayer for forgiveness before she said, "Precious, Cooper's taking us to the barbecue at Aunt Cait's."

"Oh, boy." Kira jumped up and down. "Mommy and me are wearing red, white and blue and you can, too."

"Think I'll pass on that, sunshine."

Kira's lower lip trembled. "You not going with us?"

Cooper looked at Sky and she raised an eyebrow, daring him to break her daughter's heart—and hers.

"Yeah, I'll go." The words seemed forced out.

"Yay. Yay!" Kira danced around the barn, the dogs joining in her enthusiasm with high-pitched yaps.

"You're sneaky," Cooper said.

Sky cocked her head. "I prefer to think of it as crafty."

He shook his head. "Red, parties just aren't me."

"It's time to change that."

His eyes turned somber. "Sometimes things can't be changed."

She linked her arm through his, feeling all the resistance inside him. "And sometimes they can."

THE DAY OF THE PARTY Cooper didn't show up for breakfast, and Sky's heart sank. He couldn't let them down.

"Where's Cooper?" she asked Rufus.

"He's checking the corn. He said it's time to start harvesting."

"But not today."

Ru took a swallow of coffee. "That's what I told him. Today is a fun day, but he just rode off on Rebel."

Sky tried not to think about it, but while she dressed Kira and herself in white shorts and red tank tops, she kept thinking he'd come.

She tied blue ribbons in Kira's hair and her own, all the time listening for the back door to open.

He wouldn't let them down.

COOPER SAT IN THE bunkhouse staring at his clasped hands. The barbecue wasn't his scene. He didn't need to go. The redhead had her family. He was an outsider.

As many times as he told himself that, he couldn't make himself believe it. He'd given his word. People could say a lot of things about him, but he always kept his word.

Unable to resist, he reached in his pocket for a coin and pulled out a nickel. Tossing it into the air, he caught it, then slipped it back into his pocket. He suddenly knew he couldn't decide that way.

He stood and paced, the dogs following him. Looking down at their anxious faces, he laughed—a good hearty laugh, something he hadn't done in ages. The dogs wagged their tails, sensing his change in mood.

He'd been hiding for so long he'd forgotten what real freedom was like—the freedom to laugh, love and live. So often, he'd thought he didn't deserve those things, but every time he looked into Red's eyes he saw a light that was pulling him out of the darkness, pulling him toward her and life. Toward freedom.

But so many doubts still beat at him…

BY ELEVEN, Sky gave up. He wasn't coming. Gran and Kira were ready so she couldn't stall any longer. Etta and Rufus had already left.

"I'll bring the car around," she told Gran, and headed for the back door with a heavy heart.

As she swung it open, she jumped back. Cooper stood there, shocking her out of her malaise.

"Sorry," he said. "I didn't mean to scare you."

In clean jeans, a white shirt and dress boots, he took her breath away. Her heart did a fancy two-step across her ribs. He was clean shaven and held his hat in his hand, his eyes wary.

She placed her fists on her hips. "It's about time."

He twisted his hat. "I had some things to do."

"Yeah, right."

His eyes met hers and he grinned. "I'm here now. Are you ready?"

Suddenly she wasn't upset anymore. "Yes. I was going to bring the Lincoln around."

"My truck's out front. We can go in it."

"Sure. I'll get Kira's booster seat so I can strap her in."

In fifteen minutes they were at the party. Chance, the Southern Cross foreman, was barbecuing in the backyard. Red, white and blue balloons were everywhere, with dangling streamers. Long tables covered in red gingham plastic were placed around the yard. Drinks were iced down in large chests. Country music played in the background as people mingled and visited. The kids were running and playing. Kira immediately joined Georgie.

Renee, Judd's mother, was making sure everyone had something to drink. Sky kissed her sisters and said hello, but Cooper hung back. A lot of the townspeople were here and she knew he was nervous.

She was glad when Cait hugged him and said, "Hello, cowboy. I'm glad you came."

Cooper seemed to relax.

Maddie also hugged him. "How did Sky get you off the ranch? I never could."

"It wasn't easy," Sky replied.

Maddie cradled her baby daughter in her arms. "I'm going to put her down for a nap."

"I'll do it," Gran offered. "I haven't spent enough time with her lately."

"I'll help," Nell, Walker's aunt, said.

"The pack 'n play is just inside the door." Maddie handed the baby to Gran.

"You want me to help, Mommy?" Haley, Maddie and Walker's eleven-year-old daughter, asked.

"No, sweetie, I want you to have fun."

"Okay." Haley and another girl walked off, whispering and giggling. Sky noticed they angled toward a group of boys the same age.

After Gran went inside, Maddie said, "I'm so glad you and Cooper found a way to work together."

"Me, too." Sky glanced toward the tall cowboy. "What can I say—I was a bitch."

"And so honest about it." Maddie laughed.

The constable—Maddie's husband, Walker—strolled over and wrapped his arm around his wife's waist. Tall, dark and handsome fit him to a T. "No kids?"

"For the moment." Maddie stroked his cheek and Sky thought how nice it was they were always touching each other. How nice to be in love. "Have you seen Georgie?"

"He and Kira are playing with some of the balloons Cait gave them." Walker's gaze centered on a man walking purposely toward Judd. "Uh-oh. This can't be good."

Joe Bob Shoemaker was a loud, obnoxious fool who couldn't hold his liquor. He had a beer belly the size of a small country.

With a beer can in one hand, he waddled up to Judd. "What the hell is Yates doing here?"

Without pausing, Judd replied, "I'm wondering what the hell *you're* doing here." Judd was tall, dark and dangerous, and no one had the nerve to confront him unless they were drunk or stupid.

"I'm a well-respected neighbor." Joe Bob puffed out his chest, an accomplishment in itself.

"And a drunk," Cait added. "It's time for you to leave."

"I've been a neighbor of the Calhouns and the Belles for a long time."

"It's not something we brag about." Skylar couldn't stay silent any longer.

Joe Bob swung to her. "Now listen, missy…"

Cooper stood in a trance. Every instinct in him urged him to run back to the safe haven he had built for himself before his temper brought him down. But the moment Joe Bob turned his anger on Red, something snapped in him. No one spoke to her like that, not in front of him.

He strolled forward, his hands clenched into fists. He stopped two feet away from Joe Bob. "If you have something to say about me, say it to my face. I'm standing right here and I'm not deaf."

Everyone stopped what they were doing and stared. Even the music died away.

"I…ah…I—"

"What is it?" Cooper pressed. Once he started, he couldn't stop. This was long overdue. "I was framed by an egotistical idiot similar to yourself. I spent six months in prison until the truth was revealed. Yes, I was angry at what had been done to my life, and I took that anger out in violence. I bitterly regret that, so if you have something to say, say it now, or get out of my face and never, ever speak to Skylar in that tone of voice. Cait or Maddie, either."

Joe Bob's mouth worked, but nothing came out.

Walker gripped Joe Bob's arm and Chance took the other. "Time for you to go," Walker said.

"Now wait a minute." Joe Bob drew away, and was

about to find his voice when his wife walked up with murder in her eye.

"You stupid, stupid man. Let's go," Charlene ordered.

He followed her like a dutiful puppy.

"I'm sorry," Judd said, and then looked around at the crowd. "If anyone else has any objections, I suggest you leave now."

A lot of people shook their heads. Chance flipped on the music and the party was back on track.

Skylar linked her arm through Cooper's. "My hero." She grinned and he grinned back, all the tension leaving him.

"Maybe it is time for change," he told her.

"You got it, cowboy. And if you keep looking at me like that I'm going to kiss you."

The light in her eyes eased whatever tension was left. "I—" He broke off as Brenda Sue sashayed up, her yellow hair blinding in the sunlight.

On cue, the woman's mouth started flapping like a sheet in the breeze. "Why did everyone get so quiet? I was helping Monty cut up onions and radishes, and now I smell like an onion. Monty said he doesn't mind, so I don't, either. Honestly, he can be so sweet. Cooper!" Her eyes swung to him, and without missing a beat, she added, "My, you dress up nice, real nice, and if I wasn't crazy about Monty I might dance with you tonight. Hell, after a few beers I might dance with you anyway. You know you can never—"

"Brenda Sue," Cait interrupted in a loud voice, "aren't you supposed to be setting up the main table with the side dishes? We're almost ready to eat."

"For heaven's sake, it's the Fourth of July, take a chill pill. I—"

"Brenda Sue, I suggest you do as my wife asks without saying one more word…if you value your life and your job." Judd's voice stung like a lash and Brenda Sue stomped off to the house.

"When she gets around men, her brain short-circuits more than usual," Cait said. "Pay her no mind."

"That's my motto where Brenda Sue is concerned." Sky laughed, and Cait and Maddie joined her.

Sky squeezed Cooper's hand and they walked off. "You okay?" she asked.

"I'm fine."

"Good. I'll get Kira and we'll find a place to sit."

They filled their plates and sat with Maddie and Walker and the kids. Gran joined them and so did Chance, Etta and Rufus.

"You outdid yourself, boy," Rufus said, gnawing on a rib.

"Thanks." Chance grinned like a possum eating persimmons. "I just used some of Etta's tricks. When the guy who was supposed to cook canceled, Judd asked if I could barbecue. I said hell yeah, Etta's my aunt and I watched her for years. Besides, I didn't have a date, so I might as well cook."

"Why is that?" Etta asked, piercing him with a sharp glance.

Chance wiped his mouth with a paper napkin. "I don't know. Guess I'm waiting for Skylar to notice me."

Cooper's head jerked up, but before anyone could respond, Kira pointed a chicken leg at Chance and shouted, "No. Mommy likes Coo."

Chance lifted both eyebrows. "So that's the way it is."

"Yep," Cooper replied. "That's the way it is." The words weren't just in his head; he'd said them out loud.

He wanted everyone to know. However, he was more shocked than anyone. He'd always kept his feelings hidden, but Red was changing him. For the better.

She reached for his hand under the table and he gripped it tightly. Fireworks went off inside him. It truly was the Fourth of July.

KIRA FELL ASLEEP on Cooper's shoulder about eight. Sky tried to take her, but he said she was fine. Sky gently woke her as Chance and the cowboys started a fireworks display.

Kira scrubbed at her eyes and turned around to watch. Georgie squeezed in between Sky and Cooper.

"Look, Kira, look." He pointed to the sky.

"Aahs" and "oohs" echoed for about fifteen minutes, and then Georgie glanced at Sky. "Can Kira spend the night at my house?"

"I don't know. She's never—"

"Please, Mommy. Please," Kira begged.

Maddie and Walker joined them. "We're leaving. It's time to put Val to bed."

"Mommy, Kira can come, can't she?" Georgie enlisted his mother's help.

"That's up to Aunt Sky."

"Kira's never spent a night away from me."

"Mommy, please." Kira continued to beg. "We gonna play camp out. I'll be good."

"It will be fine," Maddie said. "If she needs you, I'll call."

"She has nothing to sleep in."

"I'll find something of Haley's or Georgie's."

"If—"

Maddie cut her off. "I have liquid Tylenol."

"Okay…" It wasn't easy to let her child go, but Sky forced herself to smile.

After hugs and kisses, Kira ran off with Georgie, laughing.

"Don't worry," Maddie called over her shoulder.

Sky leaned against Cooper, needing his strength.

"We'll go get her later if you want to," he murmured.

"Thanks. I needed to hear that. I can go get her anytime I want."

The dancing started and she and Cooper danced close together. They didn't speak. They didn't need to. Their movements were in sync and Sky soaked up the tangy scent of his skin and the power of his muscles. Everything about the evening was so right.

A few minutes later they said goodbye to Cait and Judd and went home. They helped Gran inside, and then Sky was startled when Cooper said good-night and disappeared out the door. She didn't know what she was expecting, but definitely something more. Her body wanted more. *She* wanted more.

She showered and changed into an old cotton T-shirt. The house seemed so quiet without her daughter. How would she survive without her? Ever since she was born, Kira had been Sky's whole life. She'd forgotten about herself and concentrated on her child.

Now here she sat, alone.

But she wasn't alone.

She had Cooper.

She grabbed a thin cotton robe, slipped her cell phone into the pocket, crept down the stairs and out the door. The warm night air embraced her with the sweet scent of crepe myrtles and…what was that smell? Cow manure! *Oh, God, welcome to my life.*

A giggle left her throat as she stared out at the inky blackness of the night. Lightning zigzagged across the sky with a warning of rain—a much-welcomed rain. They hadn't had any in weeks, and hadn't wanted any while they'd been harvesting the hay. With a good rain now they could get a second cutting.

The moon was hidden in the vast blackness, so seeing was a little difficult, but she could probably find her way blindfolded.

As she rounded the corner of the bunkhouse she saw the porch light was on, the dogs on guard. They rose as they saw her and then wagged their tails, gazing into the darkness as if Kira might materialize.

"Sorry, guys. She's not coming tonight."

Sky took a breath and knocked on the door.

Cooper swung it open, and the coolness of the air-conditioning was as welcome as his smile. He wore nothing but a pair of jeans that rode low on his hips. Her heart kicked against her ribs.

"Oh," she murmured. "Are you going to bed?"

"Yes." He pulled her inside and closed the door.

CHAPTER TEN

SKY RAN HER PALM along his bare, damp shoulder. "You were so sure I'd come."

"If I know one thing about you, Red, it's that you're not shy." Cooper's hands locked behind her back and pulled her closer against his body.

She moved against him, feeling him respond. Kissing his chest, she asked, "Cowboy, are these muscles custom-made?"

"You bet they are—from a lot of hard work."

Her arms crept around his neck and her fingers tangled in the thick hair at his nape. She pulled him toward her and rose on her tiptoes to meet his kiss.

Their lips melted in a fiery explosion of need. She opened her mouth, offering him anything he wanted. He groaned, taking and giving with the same intensity. Tongues mingled and danced, and the heat from their bodies rivaled the heat of the day. He pulled her closer and she felt every muscle, every sinew imprinted upon her starved body—hungry for his touch and the wild sweetness it generated. The kiss went on, and their breathing became labored as their passion mounted.

Swinging her into his arms as if she weighed no more than Kira, Coop strolled to the bedroom. Though her senses were spinning, Sky noticed there weren't any bunk beds, just a king-size one. The lamp on the night-stand cast a soft glow in the sparse room. After that, her full attention was on the man in front of her.

Kneeling on the bed, Cooper removed her robe and lifted the T-shirt over her head. He took in her smooth white skin and the sprinkling of freckles across her breasts.

"Oh my God. You…you take my breath away." He gently laid her down and bent over her, licking and tasting the freckles, and then he found her nipples. Pleasure shot through her and centered in her lower abdomen. She had trouble breathing. She had trouble thinking—not that she wanted to. She just wanted to feel.

Thunder boomed and lightning lit up the room, but Sky barely noticed, as his tongue traveled to her navel and lower. When he touched her intimately, lightning and thunder boomed throughout her whole being. Her breath came in wispy gasps and his lips found hers once again. After a long, searing kiss, he said, "It's been a long time for me, Red. I don't think I can wait…." His voice was hoarse. Seductive.

"It's been a long time for me, too, cowboy, so I suggest we get you out of those tight jeans." Her hand went to the button and then she slowly unzipped them. His bulge was very evident and she slipped her hand inside his briefs.

At her touch, he moaned, lay back and shimmied out of the jeans. She caught her breath at the sheer beauty of him—all lean, sculpted and throbbing male. She bent over and ran her fingers through the golden chest hairs and followed them to his navel and below. "Oh, cowboy," she breathed as she touched and caressed every inch of his hardness.

He flipped her over onto her back. "You're driving me crazy," he said a moment before he claimed her lips and pressed his naked frame against her. Lips on lips, heart on heart, Sky felt the world float away as tortured moans echoed through the room.

Rain pelted the tin roof with a rhythmic and soothing sound that heightened the emotions, the senses. She ran her fingers through Coop's hair, moaning with each jolt of pleasure his lips and caresses created. She opened her legs and he moved between them and thrust deep inside her. Each thrust produced its own fireworks display of psychedelic lights that ended in rippling waves of pleasure.

"Red..." he whispered hoarsely as his body convulsed against her, joining her in an array of feelings as real and basic as they could get.

Nothing was said for a while as they lay there, hearts pounding. Both were exhausted. Cooper held Red against him, not wanting to let go, not wanting to let this moment end. He moved to her side and continued to hold her. She nuzzled his shoulder, and drifted into peaceful sleep.

He brushed the damp curls from her forehead and wanted to say those magic words. Words she deserved to hear. But he'd never said them to anyone, and they were buried so deep inside him he didn't know if he'd ever be able to.

She deserved a better man than that, and he knew he'd crossed a line tonight—making love with his boss. There was no going back, nor did he want to. He just had to find the courage to accept this wonderful woman into his life.

What did he have to offer her? That question tore at him, but he pushed it aside. Tonight he would enjoy this moment. And her.

He followed her into sated slumber. The buzz of a phone woke them. Red jumped out of bed and grabbed her robe, fishing her phone from the pocket.

Looking at the caller ID, she said, "Oh, no. It's Maddie. It has to be about Kira."

Sky quickly clicked on. "Maddie, what is it?"

"Kira woke up crying. Her knee is red and swollen. I gave her some Tylenol but she's not settling down. I think the lightning and thunder scared her. She wants her mommy."

"I'll be right there. Tell her Mommy is coming."

"I will."

Sky turned to search for her T-shirt and Cooper handed it to her. He was fully dressed. "Let's go," he said.

She slipped on her robe and they hurried out the door. Light rain pelted them as they ran to his truck. Within minutes they were in front of the Walker house. Sky darted in and the sight of Kira's tearstained face tugged at her heart.

Gathering her child into her arms, she said, "Mommy's here, precious." Maddie handed her a raincoat to hold over them. Sky waved goodbye and joined Cooper in the truck.

Kira wouldn't let her go, so she wrapped the seat belt around both of them. In normal circumstances she would never do this, but she'd left Kira's seat at home. She kissed her forehead, which felt warm. "I think she might have a fever."

"Do you want to go to the emergency room in La Grange?"

"No. We've been through this before. If she doesn't feel better by morning, I'll take her."

Sky smoothed back the red curls. "Look, precious. Cooper's here."

Kira raised her head from Sky's chest, scrubbing at her eyes. "Coo, I don't feel good."

Cooper's throat closed up. He swallowed hard. "I know, sunshine. We'll be home soon."

He parked in front and became very aware that he was the hired hand. His place was in the bunkhouse, not in the main house.

"I want Coo," Kira cried, and held out her arms.

He swallowed again and took her, cradling her small body. "Let's get you to bed and you'll feel better."

"'Kay."

He followed Sky into the house without a second thought, carrying Kira as if she was the most valuable thing in the world, which she was.

In the bedroom, Sky took her and laid her down, then stuck a device in her ear to take her temperature. "It's a hundred and two," she said a moment later. "I'll give her a cool bath and maybe that will bring it down."

Cooper thought that maybe he should leave, but he didn't. Red and Kira needed him.

Sky removed Kira's T-shirt and panties and carried the child to the bathroom across the hall. Kira didn't like the cold water and cried for Coop.

He knelt by the tub, stroking her hair. "I'm right here, sunshine. Just a few more minutes and you'll feel better."

"I wanna go to bed, Coo. Please."

He glanced at Red and she nodded, so he plucked the child out. Red wrapped her in a fluffy towel, and in the bedroom, slipped a gown over Kira's head. Then Cooper laid her gently in the bed.

Kira nodded off to sleep quickly, and Red examined

her knee. "It's really swollen. I shouldn't have let her run so much today, but it's hard. She wants to be like other kids and I…"

Coop heard the tears in her voice. He pulled the sheet over Kira and gathered Red into his arms. "She's a kid and she wants to play. You did nothing wrong."

"It's so hard to see her like this. It's just so unfair…."

"Shh." He gently rocked her in his arms. "She'll be better in the morning, and if she isn't, we'll see a doctor."

Red wrapped her arms around him. "Thank you. She's been my responsibility for so long, and like I said, I'm so afraid I'm doing something wrong."

"You're not." He cupped her face. "Get some rest and I'll see you in the morning." He kissed her and headed for the door.

"Cowboy."

He stopped and turned.

"Thanks for…tonight."

He grinned. "You're welcome."

When he walked out, Sky wrapped her arms around her waist. She'd always been independent, never needing anyone, but tonight she'd needed Cooper in more ways than she ever thought possible. In that moment she knew she loved him, probably had for a very long time.

For someone who'd said she'd never fall in love, it was the easiest thing in the world.

With the right man.

With Cooper.

COOPER WAS UP EARLY and checked to see how much rain the ranch had gotten. The gauge said three inches. He and Red hadn't even noticed. A lot of leaves and broken limbs were scattered about, so there had to have been high winds, too. Last year the drought had been bad, but this rain would sustain them for a while.

While he waited for the lights to come on at the house, he fed Sassy. The heifer was now in the corral and walking fine, but he still wanted her to get stronger before he introduced her back into the herd. Animals tended to prey on the weak.

While he was at it, he fed Solomon, so the animal wouldn't feel inclined to jump out of his pen. Out of the corner of his eye he saw movement. Etta was walking from her cabin to the ranch house to fix breakfast. He quickly followed.

The housekeeper looked up as she was tying her apron. "Cooper, you're early. I haven't even started breakfast."

"That's okay. I just wanted to check on Kira. We had to pick her up from Maddie's because she wasn't feeling well." He headed for the stairs.

"You can't go up there. Everyone is still asleep."

"Don't worry about it."

"Cooper…" Etta followed him like a pesky mosquito. He held a finger to his lips and went on up.

"Things sure are changing," Etta muttered as she went back to the kitchen.

He tapped lightly on Red's door. She opened it almost instantly. Her face was pasty-white and she held her cell in her hand.

"What's wrong?" He glanced at the bed and saw Kira was sleeping soundly.

"I…I got a call from the lady I rented an apartment from in Tennessee."

"And…?"

"She said her sister broke her hip, and she left soon

after I did, to take care of her. She stayed longer than she'd planned. When she returned, her husband, Norman, told her someone had ransacked my old apartment. Norman's very cheap and he was waiting for her to get back to clean it out so he could rent it again."

"But that was months ago."

"Yeah. Norman gives cheap a new meaning. He'd rather lose the rent instead of paying someone to clean it."

"What do you think it means?"

"That the Spencers are still looking for us."

"But what could they find in an empty apartment?"

"I don't know. It's a one-room furnished, and Helen said the sofa cushions and the mattress were tumbled about. Every drawer had been opened."

That anguished look on Red's face tightened his gut. Coop took her in his arms. "Try not to worry. I'll make sure no one gets close to you or Kira."

She rubbed her face against him. "I want to run like I always do."

His heart contracted. "No. You have to fight this. Call Judd. He knows a lot of people in Austin. You need to get a lawyer."

She drew back. "Yes. I can't keep dragging Kira around the country. I have to face this, just like my dad always said."

"And I'll be right here beside you."

She smiled. "Ah. It always helps to have a cowboy on my side."

He kissed her gently and then their emotions took over. Resting his forehead against hers, he whispered, "Please don't think about leaving."

She touched his face. "I won't."

NO POSTAGE
NECESSARY
IF MAILED
IN THE
UNITED STATES

BUSINESS REPLY MAIL

FIRST-CLASS MAIL   PERMIT NO. 717   BUFFALO, NY

POSTAGE WILL BE PAID BY ADDRESSEE

THE READER SERVICE
PO BOX 1867
BUFFALO NY 14240-9952

Play the Lucky Hearts Game

and get...
2 FREE BOOKS and
2 FREE Mystery GIFTS...
YOURS to KEEP!

Yes! I have scratched off the gold card. Please send me my *2 FREE BOOKS* and *2 FREE Mystery GIFTS* (gifts are worth about $10). I understand that I am under no obligation to purchase any books as explained on the back of this card.

Scratch Here!
Then look below to see what your cards get you...2 Free Books & 2 Free Mystery Gifts!

We want to make sure we offer you the best service suited to your needs. Please answer the following question:
About how many NEW paperback fiction books have you purchased in the past 3 months?
❑ 0-2   ❑ 3-6   ❑ 7 or more

❑ I prefer the regular-print edition   ❑ I prefer the larger-print edition
336 HDL EZV7   135 HDL EZWV   339 HDL EZWK   139 HDL EZW7

FIRST NAME   LAST NAME

ADDRESS

APT.   CITY

STATE / PROV.   ZIP/POSTAL CODE

Visit us online at
www.ReaderService.com

Twenty-one gets you
2 FREE BOOKS and
2 FREE MYSTERY GIFTS!

Twenty gets you
2 FREE BOOKS!

Nineteen gets you
1 FREE BOOK!

TRY AGAIN!

▼ DETACH AND MAIL CARD TODAY! ▼

® and ™ are trademarks owned and used by the trademark owner and/or its licensee.

© 2009 HARLEQUIN ENTERPRISES LIMITED. Printed in the U.S.A.

(H-SR-09/09)

"How's Kira?"

"She woke up twice, so she'll probably sleep until noon."

He stared at the red curls peeping out from the sheet. "Is her fever down?"

"Yes."

"I'll take care of the ranch. You take care of Kira." He kissed her again. "Call Judd, and I'll see you later."

"Cooper?"

He turned back and saw the fear in her beautiful blue eyes. "Come on, Red. You're stronger than this."

She blinked back a tear. "Yes, I am. Thanks for reminding me. The Spencers are not taking my child."

"No way in hell."

"I'VE LOCATED Skylar Belle and the child," Leo Garvey said into his cell phone.

"Where?" Jonathan Spencer demanded.

"In High Cotton, Texas, on the High Five ranch."

"But you looked there."

"Twice, actually. The first time a Caitlyn Belle was running the family ranch. When I went back, Madison Belle was. But this time I talked to several townspeople and they say Skylar Belle is there with her daughter."

"Have you seen her?"

"No. I thought you didn't want me to make contact."

"I don't, but I want to be sure."

"She is, but if I poke around any more she'll get wind and run. Right now she's on the ranch."

"How do we get there?"

"Your best bet would be to fly into Austin, rent a car and drive to High Cotton."

"Where in the hell is that?"

"It's barely a stop in the road in rural central Texas. I'll fax directions."

"Fine, and, Garvey? Do not let her leave."

"This is a small place and I can't fade into the background, but I will keep an eye on the entrance to High Five."

"We'll book a flight and I'll be in touch."

"So he finally found her," Cybil said as he clicked off.

"Yes. I'm calling our attorney to make sure we can take our granddaughter when we arrive."

"Everything is all set. I've hired a nurse and a nanny and I've looked into several prestigious boarding schools for when she's older."

Jonathan stared at his phone.

"What?"

"The child doesn't even know us."

"She'll adapt. Kids do."

"It seems so…"

"Don't get sentimental now." Cybil brushed off his concerns. "You know what's going to happen if we don't do something."

SKY HAD A HORRIBLE DAY. Kira was fussy and cried for ages, wanting to be held. Sky rocked her, played with her, but nothing worked. Finally, at two in the afternoon, she fell asleep. It was the worst feeling in the world, to watch her child in pain.

While Kira slept, she called Judd, who gave her the names of several lawyers. By four o'clock she'd hired Sheila Dunbar, who told her to call the moment she heard from the Spencers. Judd had said she was a tiger in the courtroom, and Sky felt a surge of confidence having someone like that on her side.

Money was a problem, and she'd told Ms. Dunbar

that. The attorney said to mail her a hundred dollars as a retainer, and that they would discuss money when the Spencers made a move.

Sky was staring at her cell phone when it buzzed. Picking it up, she glanced at the caller ID. She didn't recognize the number and was hesitant about answering, but finally clicked on. "Hello."

"Red?"

"Cooper." She sat bolt upright. "Where did you get a cell phone?"

"I had to go to Giddings to meet the man who's going to harvest the corn, so I stopped and bought one. If you need me, you can reach me at any time."

"Oh, Cooper. I…"

"What?"

She cleared her throat and said the words that were in her heart. "I love you."

Silence. Dead silence.

"You don't have to say anything."

"I don't think we should have this conversation on the phone. I'll see you tonight."

She clicked off, feeling as if she'd shot their new relationship right out of the water. Her impulsiveness was one thing she couldn't change about her personality, but she didn't regret saying the words. She meant them.

Soon he'd say them, too.

She just had to be patient.

CHAPTER ELEVEN

SKY PUT KIRA TO BED at nine. Because she'd been so fussy during the day she'd sleep all night, Sky suspected. After reading to her for a few minutes, she saw that her baby was out, but she sat with her for a long time just to make sure she was sleeping peacefully.

Cooper had come by in the afternoon, perking Kira up tremendously. Sky did notice that her child became more of a baby when Cooper was around. Kira obviously missed having a father. Sky never realized that until now.

Leaving the bedroom door open, Sky hurried downstairs. Cooper hadn't come in for supper and she had to see him.

"Gran, would you mind listening for Kira? I'm taking Cooper his supper. I'll only be a minute."

Her grandmother clicked off the TV in the parlor. "Have you and Cooper had an argument?"

"No. He's just busy."

Gran stood and walked to her, her eyes serious. "You know Kira is growing attached to Cooper."

"Yes." Sky kissed her grandmother's cheek and whispered, "And so is her mother."

"Oh, my baby." Gran hugged her. "That's wonderful."

"It is." Sky smiled. "I'll only be a minute. Call if she wakes up."

"Don't worry. I'm on duty."

"Thanks, Gran."

Sky grabbed fried chicken, rolls and what was left of the peach cobbler, wrapped it and tucked it into a picnic basket. Then she was out the door.

The moon was bright. Every time she saw its brilliance she thought of her father, and knew he was also wearing the huge gold medallion and watching over her.

Rounding the corner, she broke into a run. The dogs met her and she jogged up the steps. Before she could knock, the door opened and Cooper pulled her inside.

Tonight he wore a bathrobe, his hair wet from a shower. His arms encircled her waist and he pulled her to him. After a long, knee-wobbling kiss, he asked, "How's Kira?"

"She's asleep. I can't stay long." Sky's tongue found his bare shoulder and then his neck.

He groaned and cupped her face, kissing her deeply. She dropped the basket, but didn't care. They sidestepped, turned and shuffled down the hall to the bedroom, their lips never losing contact. Between more heated kisses, Sky's clothes were a heap on the floor with Cooper's robe.

In a minute the two of them were on the bed, their naked bodies entwined. His hands and lips found all those secret places that drove her crazy. When his tongue touched her intimately, she moaned and arched her spine. His lips trailed a path of warm fire up to her navel, her breasts and to her neck.

"I'd say 'whoa, cowboy,' but I don't think you have an off switch," she breathed with a ragged sigh. "And neither do I."

He chuckled deep in his throat.

Her hands stroked him teasingly. "I love these muscles, especially this one." She grasped his bulging manhood.

"Easy," he groaned then rolled onto her. The fireworks display began.

Later, he rested his face in the warmth of her neck, while she stroked his hair. "Is it always going to be like the Fourth of July with us?" she asked.

He raised his head and kissed her bruised lips. "Yes."

"Do we *have* an 'always'?"

Cooper drew away and sat on the side of the bed. He'd known this was coming and he wanted to explain how he felt.

"I care about you and Kira more than anyone, but…"

"But what?"

"I don't have anything to offer you. I'm the hired hand, with a prison record."

"That doesn't matter to me. You were framed by that idiot Everett."

Coop felt the bed move as she came up behind him. Her arms went around his chest and she locked her hands over his heart. "This is what I want. Your love. Your heart. You've already opened it to Kira and me. Just keep letting us in. Don't shut us out." She kissed the side of his neck. "I can be patient."

"Red." He took a long breath. "When I was in prison, I felt alone, angry and trapped. The only bright spot was recreation time in the yard. The guys tried to mess with me, but I'm a big guy and they learned quick to leave me alone. I'd sit and stare at the sky. No one bothered me because I think they concluded I was crazy and dangerous. I'd stare at that blue expanse and it calmed and soothed me. That blue represented freedom, and that's what I clung to. Your eyes are the same blue. I see freedom in their depths, but it's not easy for me."

"Oh, Cooper." She wrapped her arms around his neck and just held him.

He leaned his head back, feeling her love, her spirit and her heart. Why was this so hard? Because he wanted to offer her the world, her heart's desire, anything she wanted. But he had nothing. And that hurt more than he'd ever imagined.

She kissed the side of his face. "Did I mention that I can be patient?"

"You shouldn't."

She playfully tapped his shoulder. "I love you and I'm going to wait forever, so just keep looking in my eyes."

"Red…"

"I've got to go." She scrambled to gather her clothes and slipped into them. He watched as the moonlight splayed across her fair skin. She was so beautiful. "Your supper is on the floor in the other room." Leaning over, she kissed his lips. "I love you just the way you are, with your bruised heart, scarred soul and gorgeous body. Most of all I love you because you touched a part of me no one ever has—my conscience. And I saw the real man behind all those scars." She kissed him one more time. "I'll see you in the morning—bright and early."

At the door, she looked back. "Don't analyze everything to death. Let's take one day at a time, cowboy."

"I'm not a big analyzer."

"Yeah, right."

"Red?"

She swung back.

He reached for a piece of paper on the nightstand and handed it to her. "It's a check made out to you. The amount is blank. Use whatever you need to pay the lawyer."

"Oh, Cooper...I can't..."

"Yes, you can. Please."

She stared at him for a moment, her eyes clouded, and then she took the check and quickly left. He reached for his robe and slipped into it on his way to the kitchen. It was a minor thing, but it was important to him. She had to fight to keep Kira.

Picking up the basket from the floor, he placed it on the table.

One day at a time, Red.

That he could handle.

THE NEXT COUPLE OF DAYS were nerve-racking. Kira was better and wanted to go outside and play. But she had to rest her joints, something hard to explain to a four-year-old. She cried and cried until Cooper took her out on horseback.

He placed Kira in front of him and they went to look at the herd, the dogs following. An hour later, they returned and the little girl was happy. She had to call Georgie to tell him she'd been herding cattle.

But today Kira was again fussing to go outside.

"Baby, play with your dolls and Cooper will take you riding later."

"Why can't he come now?"

"Because he's working."

"I wanna play with the doggies."

"The dogs are with Rufus, checking the herd."

Her bottom lip trembled. "That's my job."

Kira sat on the parlor rug, her dolls strewn around her. Sky squatted to face her. "Precious, Cooper is making plans to harvest the corn and Rufus is making sure the cattle have enough water in the heat. This afternoon when it's cooler you can go riding with Cooper. But right now Mommy wants you to play with your dolls. Gran is upstairs looking for old hats to play movie stars. You'll like that."

"Uh-huh."

Sky kissed her cheek. "Mommy loves you."

"I love you, too."

"You play and Mommy will be in the study working on the books."

"'Kay."

Sky had been working about five minutes when Kira came strolling in. "Mommy, is it time yet?"

She took a patient breath. "Not yet."

Kira angled toward the window and stood there staring out, looking so lonely. Sky was at a loss on what to do. Kira couldn't run around in the yard. Sky wanted to keep her quiet for a few more days to give her knee more downtime, especially since thunderstorms were in the forecast.

Before she could find the right words, Kira said, "I'm gonna go play."

"Thank you, precious."

Sky didn't know what brought that on, but she was hoping her daughter would now settle down.

Cooper's check was on the desk and she placed it inside the ranch ledger. She would use it only if necessary. Her heart swelled with love at his concern and generosity.

Ten minutes later, the parlor seemed very quiet. She stood to go see what Kira was doing, but the phone rang.

It was Mr. Bardwell, the man who bought sand and

gravel from the ranch. He should have been on the property a month ago, but due to the poor economy he was just now planning to start. Sky told him that was fine, and hurried into the parlor.

Kira wasn't there, though her dolls and doll clothes were. Sky wasn't worried. Since Cooper had installed the latches on the doors, Kira couldn't get out. She had to be somewhere in the house.

Gran came down the stairs with two hats in her hand.

"Gran, is Kira upstairs?"

"No. Why?"

"She's not in the parlor. I'll check the kitchen."

She couldn't find her daughter anywhere in the house. Sky suspected she was hiding, until she stopped dead in the entry hall. A dining room chair was in the entry and a broom was in a corner. The latch was undone.

That little devil.

"How did she get the broom?"

"I left it there this morning when I swept the veranda," Etta said. "I was going to go back and tackle the spiderwebs. Lordy, I'm sorry, Sky."

"It's not your fault."

Sky yanked open the door. "Kira Dane Belle, you're in so much trouble." But only quiet answered her words. She ran to the barn, but Kira wasn't there. She dashed to the bunkhouse and noticed the dark clouds rolling in, easing the heat of the day. A clap of thunder echoed in the distance. Wind whistled through the trees and she knew the storm wasn't far away. She had to find her daughter.

Fifteen minutes later an eerie disquiet slid up her spine and she reached into her pocket for her cell.

"Hey, Red," Cooper said as he clicked on.

"Come home, please," she choked out.

"I'm on my way. Tell me what's wrong."

"I can't find Kira and I'm getting scared. A storm is coming and…"

"Calm down. I'm not far from the house. We'll find her."

It seemed like an hour, but Sky knew it was only a few minutes before Cooper galloped into the yard. He swung from the saddle and she quickly told him what had happened.

"She figured out a way to unlock the door?"

"Yes, and now she's probably scared and hiding from me. She'll answer you."

Cooper begged and pleaded into the wind, promised to take her riding, but Kira didn't make an appearance.

Sky ran her hands up her sweaty arms. "Coop, I'm scared. Something's wrong."

He hugged her for a moment. "I agree. I have a strange feeling, too." As he spoke, another clap of thunder echoed. "The rain will be here soon. We have to find her."

"Sky, there's a phone call for you," Etta shouted from the back door.

She ran for the house, with Cooper on her heels. Taking a deep breath, she picked up the receiver. "Hello."

"Sky, this is Nell."

Her heart sank. This was probably about High Five's bill at the general store. She didn't want to talk about that right now.

"Nell—"

"I just wanted to let you know that something looks suspicious."

"What?" Sky had no idea what the woman was talking about. She had to find her child.

"There was a black car and a sedan parked to the side of my store. Two men in suits were standing outside talking. They drove away and I asked Luther if he knew who they were. He said one man was in here last week asking about the High Five ranch and Skylar Belle."

What?

The Spencers had found her.

It took a moment for her to breathe.

"Why in the hell didn't Luther mention this last week?"

"He said the man was dressed different, in jeans and a work shirt. Said he was looking for hay and he'd heard High Five had some to sell. Then he asked if Skylar Belle was the owner. I'm sorry, Sky, poor Luther didn't think."

"How long ago were they there?"

"I don't know. I had several customers in here, and when I was free, I asked Luther about those people because he'd been watching them. Maybe twenty minutes."

Twenty minutes!

Sky dropped the phone and Cooper was immediately at her side.

"What is it? Red, talk to me."

"Those sons of bitches!"

"What?"

"They took my child. The Spencers took Kira. I know it." Her nerves were ping-ponging off each other. She couldn't think. But she had to.

"Why? Why do you think that?"

She told him what Nell had said.

"Call your lawyer and I'll call Walker."

Her trembling legs wouldn't move.

"Now, Red. Now!"

She hurried to her study. Within a few minutes the parlor was full of people. Maddie and Walker arrived, with Cait and Judd behind them.

"What did the lawyer say?" Cooper caught her hand and squeezed.

"She said to call the authorities. If they took her, it's kidnapping. And to phone her if the Spencers show up."

"I've already alerted the sheriff," Walker said. "Now tell me why you think the Spencers took her."

"Kira had a bad spell with her arthritis and I was keeping her in so she couldn't run and injure her knee further. But she was feeling better and wanted to go outside and play. I wouldn't let her. While I was in the study, she pulled a dining room chair up to the door and undid the latch with a broom. She must have just run outside when they drove up. And…and they snatched her."

"Possible, Sky, but I don't think it's likely."

"Why do you say that?" she screamed at Walker. "They took my baby."

Cooper reached for her hand again and she held on tight.

"Please listen to Walker," Maddie begged.

Sky took a long breath.

"I don't think the Spencers would risk facing kidnapping charges. It's a federal offense and these people are not stupid."

"So where's my daughter? I want my baby. She's just a baby," she wailed.

Cooper gathered her into his arms. "Come on, Red. Let's fight this. If they have her, she's safe and we'll get her back. If not, then we have a whole other problem."

"I've never been this afraid in my life."

"I'm right here. Your family is here."

She pushed back, gaining strength from him. "What do we do?"

"I have a deputy running a check on the Spencers, trying to find a phone number so we can contact them. I need a picture of Kira."

"I'll get one," Gran said from the doorway.

Oh, God, what this must be doing to her grandmother! But Gran seemed very strong as she rushed up the stairs.

"Do you have an address for them?"

"They live in New York and the family owns a pharmaceutical company, that's all I know."

"I'll get this to the deputy and maybe he can locate them."

Etta hurried in, twisting her hands. "A black car is driving up."

Sky made a dive for the front door, but Cooper caught her. "Let Walker handle it."

"I...I—"

"Listen to him," Cait said. "You need to keep a cool head."

"She's not your child," Sky fired back.

"I love Kira, too." Cait's voice wobbled.

"We all love Kira," Maddie said. "Let's don't argue. This is too important. We have to stick together."

"I'm coming apart at the seams," Sky admitted, and her sisters hugged her. "But I have to face these people."

"Just don't go all red alert, okay?" Cait stepped back and Sky and Cooper followed Walker to the door.

A man in his fifties, dressed in a suit, got out and opened the back door of the Lincoln Town car. Jonathan and Cybil Spencer stepped out, blinking at the dark clouds.

But there was no Kira.

Where was her child?

CHAPTER TWELVE

SKY TRIED TO REMAIN CALM, but she couldn't. These people were out to destroy her. Jonathan Spencer stood tall and imposing in a tailored suit. He looked so much like Todd, except his brown hair was graying, giving him a distinguished appearance.

Cybil was much the same as when Sky had last seen her, at Todd's condo. She was very elegant, sophisticated, dressed in an Armani suit matching heels and purse. Diamonds sparkled in her ears and on her hands. Not one strand of her blond pageboy hairstyle was out of place. That annoyed expression on her face got to Sky and she charged around Walker before Cooper could stop her.

"Where's my daughter?" she demanded.

Walker stepped in front of her. "My name is Walker, constable of High Cotton."

The man in front inclined his head. "I'm Carl Devlin, attorney for the Spencers."

"Why do the Spencers need an attorney?"

Mr. Devlin pulled papers from the inside of his jacket. "They've filed for temporary custody of minor child Kira Dane Belle. The hearing is at eight o'clock in the morning in Giddings."

Sky gasped. How dare they!

Walker glanced through the papers. "On what grounds?"

"That my clients would be the better parents."

"You'll need more than that."

"You low-down, sneaky, conniving…"

Her angry words trailed off as Gran approached the threesome. "Skylar, where are your manners? Please invite our guests in out of the weather. It looks like rain."

Over my dead body.

When she remained silent, seething inwardly, Gran added, "Please come in and we'll have some iced tea and discuss this rationally. We all want what's best for Kira. Don't we?" Gran stared directly at Cybil.

"Of course," the woman replied, her voice hard and cold as steel.

Gran turned and everyone followed her inside.

"Gran," Sky whispered. "This is not a social gathering."

"Oh, my baby." Gran touched her cheek with a wily grin. "Haven't I taught you that you can catch more flies with honey than with vinegar?"

"We're not catching flies."

"Flies and enemies are much the same."

"I don't have a clue what you're talking about."

"Watch and learn, my baby."

Etta brought iced tea and Gran joined the group in the parlor. Her grandmother had more strength than she did. Sky wanted to rip their eyes out.

"Can they take my baby?" she asked Walker, trying to maintain a measure of control.

"Not unless they have some damn good evidence that you're a bad mother."

"They don't," Cooper stated.

"Then let's find out what they're really up to. They're acting a little too cocky."

"Where is Kira?" Sky asked, her voice unsteady. This was taking too long. She just wanted her child back.

"Let's see if we can find out."

They followed Walker into the parlor. Maddie, Cait, Judd and Etta stood to the side, watching Gran with the Spencers and their attorney, as if watching an elephant gone amok at a circus, disbelief on their faces.

"Mr. Devlin, Skylar Belle hasn't been notified of any hearing." Walker started the conversation.

The man slipped out of his jacket and loosened his tie. "How do you people stand this oppressive heat? At least it's a little cooler with the rain coming."

No one felt a need to answer the question.

Folding the jacket, he placed it on the arm of the sofa and stared at Walker. "That's why we're here. To give her notice. And of course, the Spencers would very much like to see their granddaughter."

"She's not your granddaughter," Sky shouted, losing a grip on her control.

Mr. Devlin looked straight at her. "A DNA test shows otherwise."

"How…how—" His words took the air from her lungs. How did they get Kira's DNA? She hadn't approved that.

"If you obtained her DNA illegally—"

Mr. Devlin cut Walker off. "I assure you everything is legal."

"Where's my child? You had no right to take her." Sky's nerves snapped. She wanted these people out of her house and out of her life.

The lawyer lifted an eyebrow. "That's the second

time you've asked that. Am I right in assuming you don't know where your child is? I believe that's called neglect."

"And she hasn't been taught to pick up her toys, either." Cybil nudged a Barbie doll with the toe of her high-heeled shoe.

Before Sky could string all the angry thoughts in her head into a sentence, Gran stood, her back straight. "Skylar gives Kira the freedom to learn and grow, and she's very strict about Kira picking up her toys at the end of the day. After I offered you hospitality, you have a nerve coming into my home and criticizing my granddaughter. She's an exemplary mother raising her child alone after your perfectly raised son walked out on her." Gran stepped closer to Cybil. "I've been a Southern lady all my life, but if you don't tell us where that child is, I'm going to slap you six ways from Sunday."

Cybil rose, indignation in every move. "How dare you."

Gran lifted a hand, and obviously Cybil thought she was going to strike her. She fell backward into the chair, her mouth working, but no words came out.

Cait and Maddie immediately went to Gran, one on each side of her. "Calm down, Gran," Cait said.

She shook them off. "I'm not calming down until they tell us where Kira is. It's despicable to steal a child."

The lawyer rose to his feet. "This is getting out of hand. We do not have the child. I repeat, we do not have Kira Belle. That would be kidnapping and I would not allow my clients to do that when we can easily win in court."

A moan left Sky's throat. If they didn't have her…

"You'd better be telling the truth," Cooper said.

"I am."

They walked out into the foyer. Cait and Maddie stayed with Gran, who'd obviously forgotten about the flies and honey thing.

"What do you think?" Cooper asked Walker.

"I believe them. We have to scour every inch of this ranch. I'll call for volunteers. Kira has to be here."

"She's tiny and could hide anywhere. I'll start in the barn again." Cooper rushed out the door.

Sky was in limbo. Her nerves were frayed and she just wanted to sit and cry, but she didn't. With her sisters' help, she checked every inch of the house again, even the attic.

The Spencers watched from the parlor, sipping tea. Gran was with them, but no one said a word. They didn't want to rile her.

The Belle sisters met the guys at the barn. Cooper swung into the saddle. "We'll spread out and search around the property," he announced. Sky noticed her horse was saddled, and she grabbed the reins.

Cars and trucks came to a stop outside the barn. The people of High Cotton had come to help.

Cooper watched as they all gathered round: Skully, Joe Bob, Charlie, and even Luther, who always looked down his nose at Coop when he picked up feed. But today wasn't about him. It was about finding Kira.

Rufus rode in, the dogs trailing behind him. "What are all these people doing here?"

"Kira's missing," Cooper told him.

"She's just adventurous. She's probably hiding in the loft."

"We've checked...everywhere."

"Good God." Rufus pulled his hat low. "What's the plan?"

"We're..." Coop glanced down and saw only two dogs. "Where's Boots?"

"That lazy thing must have come back to the house," Rufus replied. "I was checking the pasture by the house, where we put those heifers, and I noticed he was gone."

Cooper turned to Sky. "Was Kira looking out a window?"

"Yes. She was moping and then she got all excited. Oh, no."

Cooper kneed his horse and shot out of the barn, Sky and the others right behind him. He spurred Rebel on and pulled up when he reached the site of the old abandoned well. *No!* The boards lay in the grass again and the ground was rooted up. Clearly, the hogs had been here before they'd trapped them. Even after the rain, the damage was visible. They'd pried the boards loose and the rain had caused the sand he'd dumped into the well to sink. He could see a hole.

He dismounted, searched his saddlebags for a small flashlight and moved toward the well. His insides coiled into a tight knot. The hole was about three feet wide, but he couldn't see how deep. As he stepped closer, dirt crumbled around the edges.

Shit!

Riders dismounted behind him. "Stay back," he shouted. Out of the corner of his eye, he saw Maddie's SUV stop, and she and Cait got out. More townspeople arrived as Cooper concentrated on the hole.

He glanced at Walker and Judd. "Keep everyone back."

How did he get to the hole without it caving in? Was Kira inside? *God, please, no!*

Removing his hat, he fell to his knees and lay flat on

the warm ground, inching his body along like a lazy snake toward the opening, testing the ground to see how much weight it could take.

"Cooper," Red called. "What are you doing?"

He couldn't answer, not now.

Closer and closer he inched, making sure none of the dirt shifted. Finally, he reached the edge and stretched his neck to look into the hole. Complete darkness. He swung the light forward and switched it on, his heart knocking against his ribs like a hammer. He saw white sneakers. *Oh, God, no, no!* He couldn't swallow. He couldn't breathe. And then he heard a bark.

"Boots, are you in there?"

Coop forced himself to focus. The hole was about twenty feet deep. Kira was folded in half at the bottom, her feet and head in the air, her rear below. Boots straddled her; that's all the room they had. She must have been chasing the dog and they'd fallen in.

"Kira, baby," he called, his voice raspy to his own ears. "Can you hear me? Kira! Please answer!"

No response.

His breathing became labored with the taste of fear.

"Hold on, Boots," he said, and slowly inched backward. When he was a good eight feet away, he stood, his heart heavy in his chest. How did he tell Red? Oh, God, this was his fault. After dumping the sand in the well, he should have come back to check that everything was fine. Oh, God, no!

The clouds grew darker and the smell of rain hung in the air, augmenting the fear and horror that were building inside him.

Red ran to him. "What did you find?" Cait and Maddie stood beside her, as did Walker and Judd. The townspeople waited patiently, their eyes all centered on him.

He cupped her face with his dirty hands. "Kira... Kira's at the bottom of the old well."

"No, no, no!" Sky screamed, and her cries echoed across the landscape and mingled with the thunder. Her knees buckled and he caught her, stroking her hair. "No!"

"I'll get her out."

Red raised her head from his chest, took several deep breaths while swiping at her tears. "Is she...?"

"I don't know. Boots is down there, too. He's barking, so he's alive." Coop released Sky and her sisters took her arms. "I'll get her out," he promised.

"How?" Walker asked.

"The sand is caving in, so I have to be real careful or they'll be buried alive." He glanced around. "That oak tree is too far away to help."

"We need a dragline excavator or a front-end loader," Judd said.

"We can't get close enough with a front-end loader. The weight would cause the well to cave."

"I'll see if I can find a dragline." Judd reached for his phone.

A rumble of thunder shook the sky. "Goddammit!" Cooper glanced at the darkening sky as another clap of thunder sounded. "We have to get her out quick. Time just ran out." He walked to his horse and grabbed his rope.

"What are you doing?" Walker demanded.

"I'm not sure."

Raindrops peppered their heads.

"It's already raining in Giddings," Joe Bob said, his

cell to his ear. "The storm'll be here in less than thirty minutes."

Judd slipped his cell into his pocket. "A dragline can't get here in less than two hours. Maybe more."

"That's too long. It'll be dark in two hours. We have to get her out now." Cooper turned to study the situation.

After a moment, he said, "This is how we're going to do it. First, I have to get this rope around her feet and pull her out vertically, so she doesn't bang against the sides of the well, causing it to collapse."

"How in the hell are you going to do that?" Judd asked.

Cooper didn't have time to explain. Kira's life was at stake. "Rufus, bring your rope and get Sky's off her horse."

"Maybe we should wait for the dragline," Joe Bob muttered. "This is too risky."

Cooper looked at Red. "What do you want to do?"

"Get my baby out—now. I trust you."

That's all Cooper needed to hear. He tied the ropes together, making sure the knots were secure. There was no room for error. "Pull Maddie's SUV up to there." He pointed to a spot. "Once I get the rope around Kira's feet, I can guide her up, but I'll need a couple of tall men on top of the SUV, holding the rope high to give it some height. It's too dangerous to pull it across the ground."

"Man, are you saying you're going to pull her out with your bare hands?" Joe Bob asked.

"No. Drive your truck to the back of the SUV and attach the end of the rope to the bumper. When everyone's in place, we'll slowly begin and pray like hell that it works."

"My truck has a spotlight on top for hog hunting,"

Skully said. "I'll pull it as close as I can and turn the light on. That should help, as it's starting to get dark."

"Thanks," Coop replied.

"I'll handle Joe Bob's truck." Red moved away from her sisters.

"Red…" Cooper didn't think that was a good idea.

"I have to do something."

He looked into those sad blue eyes and knew she could handle it. Skylar Belle was strong and she'd do anything to save her daughter.

"Get the vehicles in place," he shouted. "Who's guiding the rope?" Walker, Judd and Chance stepped forward. "You'll need some gloves to keep from getting rope burns."

Cooper lay on the ground again, the rope curled around one shoulder as he slowly moved forward.

"Cooper," Walker called. "You'll need a pair of gloves."

"I'll get a better grip without them." As he moved along, rain peppered his head once again. Time was running out.

He reached the hole and pulled on the rope. "Give me some slack." Instantly, it gave, and he carefully dangled a loop over the edge. He reached for the small flashlight in his shirt pocket and placed it in his mouth to shine into the hole. Skully's light helped, too. Cooper had to stretch his neck because he dared not get any closer.

Kira's feet were propped against the wall. He was going to need a miracle. Wiggling the rope slightly, he removed the flashlight and said, "Get it, boy. Get it."

Without much enthusiasm, Boots whined and sniffed the rope. The dog must be suffering from heat and dehydration, but he was Kira's only hope.

Remembering a game they played often, Cooper said, "Get the shoe." Boots had a fascination with shoes and had chewed up many of Cooper's boots. "Bite the shoe. Come on, boy. Bite Kira's shoe." He wiggled the rope.

Boots grabbed the sneaker, and as it moved, Cooper slipped the rope over it. "Great, boy. Great!" But they had one more to go.

Holding the flashlight with one hand, the rope in the other, he tried again. "Come on, boy, bite the sneaker."

Boots lay across Kira now, his head down. He didn't seem to have any energy left.

Cooper took a long breath as sweat rolled off his face. "Shoe, shoe, get the shoe," he shouted.

Boots lifted his head.

Cooper wiggled the rope. "Get the shoe! Come on, boy! Just one more time."

The dog whined and bit the same shoe.

More rain pelted Coop's head.

Goddammit!

"No, boy." He jiggled the rope again. "This one. Get it. Get it!"

Boots didn't move.

"Come on, boy. This is for Kira. Bite the shoe. Get it, boy." He swung the rope in that direction.

Boots raised his head and with a spurt of energy latched on to Kira's other sneaker. When it moved, Cooper slipped the loop over it and tightened the rope. "Good boy. Good boy." *Thank God*.

"I got her feet," he shouted. He held his arms as far out as he could over the hole and made a fork with his hands, the rope in between. "Okay, tighten the line. Slowly."

The rope became taut.

Joe Bob crouched at his feet. "Tell us what to do."

Cooper glanced over his shoulder. Walker, Judd and Chance stood on top of the SUV, their arms in the air, the rope held in their palms. Red sat in the truck, waiting for orders. Out of the corner of his eye he noticed a TV crew, but that was of no concern to him.

He had only one thought. *Please, God. Let this work.*

"Tell Sky to back up so I can get Kira vertical. Very slowly. If I shout 'fast,' that means back that truck up like hell."

Joe Bob relayed the message and the rope began to move, cutting into his hands. Coop should have taken the gloves for this part, but he didn't have time to get any. Using all his strength, he kept his arms rigid. He couldn't see, but he felt the weight. Kira was moving.

"A little faster," he shouted.

Standing outside the truck, Cait gave the message to Sky. She pressed the gas pedal and the truck moved backward. The guys on the trucks struggled to maintain their balance and keep their arms high. Joe Bob held down Cooper's feet and others supported the guys on the SUV.

Sky tried not to think. She kept her gaze on Cooper and his outstretched arms. How was he holding them so steady? Her heart hummed as loudly as the engine, and she kept looking, praying for the sight of her child.

"Faster," Joe Bob yelled, and she heard him over the roar of the motor. She pressed her foot down and the truck sped backward.

White sneakers appeared, and Cooper grabbed them, rolling away with Kira in his arms. Sky jumped out of the truck and flew back across the pasture to them. Cooper carefully laid her daughter in the grass, and Sky fell down beside her. The little one was unmoving, dirty from head to toe.

A sob chocked Sky's throat as she gathered her baby into her arms. Kira was so still, so lifeless. "Oh...oh...is she...?" Sky couldn't say the words. She just kept holding on for dear life.

Cooper removed the ropes from Kira's ankles and laid his palm flat on her chest. "She's breathing...barely. We have to get her to a hospital."

"An ambulance is on the way," Judd said as the crowd gathered around. Light rain began to fall in earnest, but no one seemed to notice.

People offered shirts and jackets to cover Kira.

And then they heard a low bark coming from the hole.

Cooper stood and grabbed the rope, dropping the loop into the well. Everyone watched as if mesmerized.

"Get it, boy. Get it," Cooper called, and Sky noticed his voice was shaky.

Thunder clapped and rain fell, but no one moved.

"Boots, get it! Damn it, bite the rope."

Evidently the dog obeyed. Cooper wrapped the rope around his arm, dug in and yanked, then wrapped the rope again and jerked, until finally Boots flew out of the hole, knocking Coop backward. The dog lay limp on top of him, the rope clenched between his teeth. Cooper hugged him, but Boots was unresponsive.

As Cooper stood, the well caved in with a swoosh.

"Oh!" The cry echoed through the crowd.

An ambulance roared into the pasture, siren blaring and lights flashing. Paramedics in slickers darted out. A minute later they had Kira loaded, and Sky followed on trembling legs. Her sisters were there to offer encouragement.

She looked back, refusing to leave without Cooper. "Cooper," she called. "We need you."

He handed the dog to Rufus. "Take care of him."

"I'll look him over," Charlie offered. "It's probably heat exhaustion." He reached for Cooper's bloody hand. "Man, I ain't never seen nothing like that."

Coop ran toward the ambulance, and Sky wondered why it had taken a tragedy for the people of High Cotton to see the real Cooper Yates.

CHAPTER THIRTEEN

"READY?" the driver asked.

"Let's go," the paramedic checking Kira called. "Her pulse and blood pressure are very low, but she's alive."

Sky brushed the dirty red curls from Kira's forehead, her hand shaking. "Wake up, precious, it's Mommy."

"We're headed for La Grange," the driver said. "It's the closest hospital."

"Let me call her doctor." Sky fished her cell out of her pocket. "My daughter has juvenile arthritis and the doctor may want her in Austin, to get proper treatment."

"Hey, sunshine." Cooper took over talking to Kira. "It's Coo. Open those beautiful blue eyes."

Sky handed the paramedic the phone. "She wants to talk to you."

"Yes, ma'am, I've already started an IV. She's very dehydrated and unresponsive. Yes, ma'am. We're on our way. I'll call if there's any change."

"She's meeting us in the emergency room." He handed Sky the phone and stared at Cooper. "Sir, your hands are bleeding."

"I'm okay. Just take care of Kira."

"Kyle," the paramedic called to his partner in the passenger seat. "I've got the baby. Take care of the gentleman."

"There's no need..." Cooper began.

"Yes, there is," Sky interrupted. "He pulled my daughter out of an old abandoned well."

"It's good to know we still have heroes."

"He's *our* hero." Sky smiled for the first time in hours.

The paramedic checked Cooper's hands. "Holy cow. What happened?"

"Just a rope burn."

Sky moved to look, and caught her breath. A strip of flesh had been torn away between his thumbs and forefingers.

Kyle cleaned and wrapped gauze around Cooper's wounds. "Have the E.R. people look at them," he instructed.

Sinking down, Sky wrapped her arms around Cooper. He buried his face in her neck. There were both wet from the rain, but neither noticed. They just needed each other.

As the ambulance rolled steadily toward Austin, Sky thought how lucky she and Kira were to have this incredible man in their lives.

"I DEMAND TO KNOW what's going on." Carl Devlin faced Walker, Judd and the group who had returned from rescuing Kira. "We've been sitting here for over an hour, waiting for news."

"Kira's been found," Walker said, wiping rain from his forehead. "She's on the way to the emergency room."

"Where?" Jonathan asked.

Walker glanced at Judd, who glanced at his wife.

"The ambulance is on the way to Austin so Kira can get specialized care." Cait stepped forward, shaking water from her hair.

"Why does she need specialized care?"

Cait paused. "You don't know, do you?"

"Know what?" Cybil asked.

"Kira has juvenile arthritis."

"Why weren't we told this?" Jonathan demanded.

"Why would Sky feel the need to tell you? Your son wants nothing to do with the child. Skylar has been raising her alone and doing a damn good job."

"Not from where I'm standing," the lawyer said. "Skylar Belle endangered her child's life by not keeping a close eye on her. This will seal our case."

"It's time for us to go." Jonathan took his wife's arm, and the trio left the room.

Once outside, Jonathan said, "We didn't know the child had medical problems."

"Does it make a difference?" Carl asked.

Jonathan glanced at his wife.

"This does change things somewhat," Cybil answered. "But no, we have to gain custody."

Their lawyer loosened his tie a little more. "Skylar Belle just made that easy."

WHEN THEY REACHED the emergency room, Kira was whisked away, a team of doctors and nurses around her. Her shorts, panties and top were cut off.

One doctor paused, noting her bruised ankles. "How did she get those?"

"She was pulled out of an old well she'd fallen into," Sky replied, then answered a barrage of other questions, until the pediatric rheumatologist, Jana Morgan, arrived.

"How is she?" Sky asked.

"I don't know yet. I'll check her and run some tests. We'll know more then."

"May I stay with her?"

"If she wakes up, I'll send someone for you. Right now we'll be working with her constantly. There's coffee in the waiting area. This won't take long."

"Dr. Morgan…"

"She's in very good hands. I promise."

Sky had no choice but to give in. She and Cooper found a small waiting room, where two couples with children were watching a TV.

Cooper took her hand and she felt the softness of the gauze. "You need to get your hands checked," she murmured.

"They're just raw and will heal quickly."

Sky rubbed his arm. "You're so stubborn."

"I can't think about anything but Kira right now."

"Me, neither. I…" Her voice trailed away as a TV announced, "Breaking news." And there was Cooper with his arms outstretched, holding the rope in place.

They sat up straight, listening to the reporter. "Daring rescue of a little girl in High Cotton, Texas. Four-year-old Kira Belle was playing unsupervised and fell into an abandoned well. The whole town pulled together to save her. There were heroic efforts by many today." The camera zoomed to the ambulance, and Cooper following her inside. "The man with Ms. Belle, Kira's mother, is ex-con Cooper Yates. The child's grandparents, Cybil and Jonathan Spencer, would like to know Ms. Belle's involvement with the ex-con."

Cybil and Jonathan appeared on the camera.

"I understand you're trying to gain custody of your grandchild," the reporter said.

"Yes," Cybil replied. "We're very concerned about our granddaughter and the company her mother keeps."

The camera flashed to the reporter. "We will update this story on the ten o'clock news." The TV went back to its regular program.

Sky sat frozen, not quite believing what she was witnessing. "Did you see a camera crew out there?"

"Yes." Cooper got up and walked out of the room.

Sky quickly followed.

His back was rigid and his face set, as she'd seen it so many times when they'd first met.

She touched his arm. "Cooper."

"You're going to lose Kira because of me."

"No. That's not true."

His eyes darkened and she could feel that invisible wall coming down between them, the one he'd erected months ago, to keep people out. She and Kira had broken through, but now...

Dr. Morgan came out and Sky ran to her. "How's my daughter?"

The doctor looked down at the chart in her hand. "Doing remarkably well, considering."

An enormous weight lifted from Sky's heart and she could actually breathe without pain.

"Given the heat, I was worried about her brain being deprived of oxygen," the doctor went on. "But all her scans are normal. I daresay if she'd been in that well much longer she would have died, but kids are very resilient. In this case, though, it's beyond anything I've ever seen."

"Oh, thank you," Sky cried.

"Amazingly nothing is broken, but she's severely bruised, especially her right knee."

"It was swollen already. That's why I was keeping her in, which she didn't like. When I wasn't looking she found a way to get outside. It was just a matter of minutes, but she was gone, chasing one of the cow dogs. That's our guess, because the dog was in the well with her."

"I guess they kept each other alive." The doctor scribbled something in the chart.

"Can I see her?"

"They're taking her to a room in the pediatric ward. You can join her there. It's a private room, because I want complete quiet for her. We'll keep an eye on her for the next couple of days just to make sure everything is okay."

"Thank you."

The doctor closed the chart. "She'll be screaming holy hell when she wakes up, so be prepared."

"How long will that be?"

"We have her on oxygen and fluids, so as soon as her oxygen levels rise and her body has enough liquid, she should wake up."

"We'll go to her room."

"Ms. Belle?"

Sky stopped and looked back.

"We'll keep her sedated and as comfortable as possible."

"Thank you."

Cooper didn't say a word on the way to the ward. Sky thought she'd wait until they got there before talking to him, but the attendants wheeled Kira in and she was at once consumed with her child.

Her baby was so pale and dirty.

"May I give her a bath?" she asked the nurse.

"A sponge bath for now. I'll bring some towels." The woman disappeared out the door.

Cooper brushed back the dirty curls. "Hey, sunshine, it's Coo. Wake up for me. Please."

Sky watched him with her daughter and knew he loved Kira. No one could have gotten her out of that hole alive but Cooper. Sky had to convince him how much they needed him.

The nurse came back and together they bathed Kira, removing most of the dirt. The little girl was still motionless, unresponsive. Sky removed dirt from her hair with a brush that was in the packet the nurse had brought.

As she worked, she remembered Kira's lost hairbrush. She couldn't find it when they'd packed to go to High Five, so Sky had bought another. Now she was wondering if they'd left it in the apartment in Tennessee. Could the Spencers have gotten Kira's DNA from that?

She told Cooper her suspicions.

"It's possible. They had to get it somewhere."

Sky caught his hand as he helped with Kira's gown. "We're not losing Kira. You told me to fight and that's what I'm doing."

"Mommy…"

"Oh, oh, baby." Sky cradled her child's face, careful not to dislodge the oxygen mask. "Mommy's here. You're okay."

Tears rolled from Kira's eyes and she began to cry, sad whimpering sounds that twisted Sky's heart.

"Hey, sunshine." Cooper touched her bruised hand.

Kira held out her arms. "Coo."

While the nurse injected something into the IV, Cooper gathered the little girl close. Kira soon relaxed and went limp, and he gently laid her back into the bed.

"She'll sleep for a while," the nurse said, then glanced at their bedraggled clothes. "You need to rest, too."

Sky ran her hands down her damp shirt. "I guess we look pretty bad."

Cooper touched his tousled hair. "I don't know where my hat is."

Her eyes met his. "You saved Kira's life. Thank you."

"The sight of her small body wedged in that hole will be forever branded on my heart." His eyes clouded from all the emotions he was feeling.

"Cooper…" She'd started around the bed when there was a knock at the door. "Come in," she called.

A woman in her late thirties or early forties, with glasses perched on her nose, and chic, short brown hair that flipped up at her nape, walked in. "Hi, I'm Sheila Dunbar. I'm looking for Skylar Belle."

"That's me."

"Great."

They shook hands.

"This is Cooper Yates." Sky made the introduction.

"Oh, yes." Ms. Dunbar took a seat in a straight-backed chair, placing her purse and briefcase at her feet. "Your picture is all over TV and the Internet."

"We saw some footage earlier," Sky said. "The Spencers are working it to their advantage."

"You bet they are, honey." Ms. Dunbar reached for her briefcase and unzipped it. "I just had a chilling meeting with Carl Devlin. He's a cutthroat attorney with an agenda, and he's working the media for all it's worth, getting the public on his side. But we don't need the public. All we need is an understanding judge."

"So you think we can win? I *can't* lose my daughter."

"Now don't you fret, honey. I've worked with lawyers like ol' Carl before, and I plan to beat him at his own game."

"How?"

"Well, I need something to blow his ass right out of the water."

Sky had never met the woman before and was really beginning to like her Texas wit and kick-butt attitude.

"Todd Spencer is our ace in the hole."

"Todd?"

"Yes. Do you have any idea where I can locate him?"

Sky shook her head. "I called a couple of times after he left, but he never answered. I called when Kira was diagnosed and left a message. He changed his number after that."

Ms. Dunbar drew a pad from her case and scribbled something on it. "Charming, just like his parents."

"He washed his hands of both of us. He made that very clear."

"Mmm." She scribbled again. "I have a crackerjack P.I. looking for the scum. I hope that's okay with you."

"Yes, but why do you want to find him?"

Ms. Dunbar pushed her glasses up with the end of her pen. "We need him on our side."

"What?"

"Don't lose your grip, honey. We just want him to relinquish his parental rights."

"Oh."

"If we can get him to do that, and sign a paper saying you're the better person to raise Kira, then we've got more than a leg to stand on."

"What if he won't?"

"If you want to keep your daughter, we have to have him on our side. It's as simple as that."

"But…"

Ms. Dunbar glanced at Cooper. "And you need to distance yourself from the cowboy...for now."

"No. Kira and I need him."

The lawyer zipped up her briefcase with sure movements. "I realize this is difficult, but you have to make hard choices...for Kira. Reporters will be looking for you, and the cowboy doesn't need to be here. Trust me on that. I will bury Carl Devlin and the witchy grandparents. You just have to trust me."

Her cell buzzed. "That's probably my P.I. I'll take it outside. I'll be in touch."

Sky's world came crashing down once again. She had to choose between Cooper and her daughter? That was so unfair. Her heart split in half and a soft moan left her throat. She wanted to fight with Cooper by her side, but now that wasn't an option.

Damn the Spencers!

She turned as Cooper kissed Kira's forehead and whispered something. She didn't hear his words, but knew what he was saying. *I love you.*

Then he walked out of the room, and Sky let him go.

She sank into a chair and cried and cried for everything she'd just lost.

COOPER SAT IN THE HALL, because he didn't have the energy to go any farther.

Ms. Dunbar had only said what he'd known all along: he was bad for Red and Kira. His past followed him everywhere, and it would only tarnish their lives, too.

Now he had to find the strength to walk away.

Before he could move, the Belle family came down the hall.

Caitlyn handed him a bag. "I braved the bunkhouse and brought you some fresh clothes…and your hat."

"Thanks." He took it from her.

"How's Kira and Sky?"

"Kira's going to be fine, but they're monitoring her very closely."

"I'm going to see my babies." Gran headed for the room and went in.

Maddie touched his arm. "Are you okay?"

"Just a little tired," he lied.

She hugged him. "Thank you." And then she followed Cait into the room. Walker and Judd hung back.

"Are you sure you're okay?" Walker asked.

The click of heels against the tiled floor caught their attention. Ms. Dunbar rounded the corner and stopped by him.

He made the introductions.

"My, my," she said, glancing from Walker to Judd. "Must be something in the water in High Cotton. Sure grow 'em tall and strong in that part of the woods."

"It's just from hard honest work, ma'am," Judd replied.

"Yeah, right." She smiled and looked at Coop. "My P.I. found Todd Spencer."

He jumped to his feet. "Where?"

"Dallas. Isn't that nice? Almost in our backyard."

"Are you going to talk to him?"

"Oh, no, hon. A lawyer would just make him nervous. I need someone to persuade him."

"Of what?" Walker asked.

Ms. Dunbar told him what she needed.

"I'll do it," Walker volunteered.

"No," Cooper said. "I will. I have to do it for Red."

Ms. Dunbar reached in her briefcase for a large

manila envelope and pulled papers from it. "Get him to sign where the tabs are, every one of them. I have no doubt you can do this, Mr. Yates." She also handed him a card and a photo. "My cell number and Mr. Spencer's hotel and room number are on the back. That's his picture. Call if you run into trouble." With that, she walked to the elevator.

"Coop, no offense, but you're already in enough trouble for leaving the county. You're on probation."

Cooper looked straight at Judd. "A few more miles isn't going to matter. I have to do this for Red and Kira."

"I'll go with you," Walker offered.

"No." Judd shook his head. "That's not a good idea. As a law officer, you could get in trouble. You know Cooper's not supposed to leave the county."

"He doesn't need to go alone."

"I'm going," Judd stated.

"So am I." Walker made his position clear. "I'm known for doing the right thing, and in this case I feel I am. If we run into problems, I can always say I was bringing him back."

"Okay." Judd turned toward the door. "Let's visit Kira and inform our wives of this new development."

"Please don't tell Red I'm going," Coop said. "She'll just worry."

Thirty minutes later they were on a plane headed for Dallas. Cooper had no idea what he was going to say to Todd Spencer, but one way or another, the man was signing away his rights.

It would be the last thing he'd do for Red and Kira.

CHAPTER FOURTEEN

THE CAB DROPPED THEM off at the entrance to the Adolphus Hotel in downtown Dallas. Cooper took in the huge skyscrapers and bright lights and knew he was out of his element. In the large foyer, with its dazzling chandeliers, fresh flowers and ornate staircase, he felt he should wipe his boots. This kind of wealth made him uneasy. Uncomfortable.

"Let's go to the Rodeo Bar and Grill," Walker suggested. "We can get our bearings and decide the best course of action."

They strolled into a room of rich tones and Old West collectibles. Neon beer signs lit up the bar and a huge TV screen was showing a baseball game.

"Man, I could use a shot of bourbon," Judd said as they sat on stools at the lacquered bar.

"One bourbon," the bartender said. "What will you gents have?" He looked at Walker and then Cooper. The kid had spiked hair, studs in his ears, and didn't look old enough to vote, much less sell liquor.

"No." Judd raised a hand. "I'd love bourbon, but I'll take a glass of ginger ale."

The boy lifted a pierced eyebrow.

"My wife's pregnant and we have... Never mind, just bring the ginger ale."

"Make that two," Walker said.

"Three." Cooper made it unanimous as he laid the manila envelope on the bar. He'd been clutching it in his hand ever since they'd left Austin.

"Cait not letting you drink?" Walker asked.

"Nah. She can't drink, so I said I wouldn't, either. I just want to keep my word."

"I'm a lawman, so that's why I'm not drinking."

"I'm not supposed to drink," Coop stated. "Although I do have beer every now and then at the bunkhouse." The bartender set a glass in front of him and he took a swig. "Hell, I'm not allowed to do much of anything. I'm not even supposed to be in a bar like this. I can't carry a firearm. I can't vote and I can't get a damn credit card."

"Forget about it," Judd said, taking a sip of his own ginger ale. "You can pay me back whenever you want to."

It still irked Coop that he couldn't pay for his own plane ticket because he didn't have a credit card. So many of his rights had been taken away. That bothered him.

But worst of all, because of his past, he couldn't love the woman who gave his life meaning. And he'd damaged her chances of keeping her child. He had to make that right.

Judd looked at his watch. "It's after twelve. Do we just knock on his door?"

"He'll be pissed and not receptive to our way of thinking." Walker tipped up his glass. "But I sure as hell don't want to spend the night."

"Me, neither," Judd said. "I'm worried how all this trauma is going to affect Cait and the baby. I need to be with her."

"Cait's strong and she'd…" Cooper's voice trailed off as he noticed a man on a stool at the end of the bar. He reached for the manila envelope and fished out the photo of Todd Spencer.

"What do you think?" He showed the others the photo and nodded toward the man, who was wearing tailored slacks with a loose-fitting shirt and sandals. His lean face had a five o'clock shadow, his blond hair was cut short. A typical tourist with money, but Cooper knew he wasn't typical. He was Todd Spencer—Kira's biological father.

"Pay dirt," Walker said under his breath. "Now…"

"I'll take it from here." Cooper slipped the photo into the envelope.

"Cooper…" But he wasn't listening to Walker. He could handle this.

"Good luck." He heard Judd's low voice as he moved away.

Cooper took the stool next to Todd Spencer, laying the envelope on the bar in front of him. "Howdy."

The man sipped his drink and didn't respond.

"May I speak to you for a minute?"

"No," Todd replied in a snooty voice. "I'm not interested in chitchat."

"It's about your daughter."

"I don't have a daughter." His words were clipped and he still didn't look at Coop.

"Her name is Kira. Skylar Belle's daughter." Coop tossed out the words like bait, waiting for him to bite. He didn't.

After a moment Todd turned his head and looked at Cooper's bandaged hands. "I saw everything on the news, so save your little speech. It's wasted on me."

"That's cold."

"It's a cold world."

Cooper felt as if he was seeing himself through a looking glass. He'd been this embittered, this scarred and unfeeling—until Red.

Turning to face Todd, he said, "Here's the deal. Your parents are trying to gain custody of your biological daughter. Do you want that to happen?"

"My parents shouldn't be allowed to raise a dog."

"Good. We're on the same page."

"We're not." Without missing a beat, he added, "Another Scotch on the rocks, Joe."

Cooper's temper kicked in, but he kept it under control. The bartender set the drink in front of Todd and Cooper grabbed it, holding it out of Todd's reach. "Look at me, damn it. I'm talking about a little girl with your DNA who is about to be taken away from a mother who loves her. Is that what you want?"

"It's not my business. Now give me my damn drink."

Cooper slid the glass in front of him. "I'm making it your business."

Todd took a big swig. "This conversation is over."

He made to rise and Cooper grabbed his forearm in a viselike grip. "Sit down or I'm going to snap your arm like a pretzel. Got it?" He didn't raise his voice or get angry. He just stated a fact.

To Cooper's surprise, Todd sank onto the stool. That was the first sign the man was a wimp.

Coop released his arm. "Now answer my question. Do you think your parents are the better people to raise Kira Belle?"

"Hell, no."

"Why?" Cooper leaned in close. "And I want an honest answer. Now."

Todd took a sip of his drink. "I had a nanny and a nurse until I was eight years old, and then I was sent away to boarding school. I spent my holidays and birthdays with the headmaster's family. I rarely saw my parents when I was at home, but during those school years I saw them about once a year. They sent gifts, but I never got their time. They were too busy living their own lives. Love is not a Spencer emotion."

"And I thought I had a crappy childhood."

Todd reached for his drink again. "Your parents couldn't be worse than mine."

"My dad beat me almost every day of my life until I learned to hide from him. I have scars on my back that will never go away." The words slipped out before Cooper could stop them.

Todd raised his glass. "Here's to lousy parents."

Cooper leaned closer. "Todd, help me help Skylar keep her baby."

"I'm not getting involved."

"Are you a wimp or a man?"

Todd shook his head. "You just don't give up, do you?"

"Don't allow Kira to be raised by your parents. You know her life will be a living hell. I'm not asking anything of you. No admission that she's yours, even though DNA already says she is. No liability. Nothing more than your signature."

"What the hell are you talking about?"

Cooper pulled the papers from the envelope. "Sign away your rights as a father, which the DNA match gives you, and sign a document stating that it is your wish Skylar Belle raise Kira. It's as simple as that. You don't want any responsibility. This is your opportunity to make it legal and wash your hands of the whole situation."

Todd fiddled with his drink. "You don't know my parents. They'll never let go of the child."

Something didn't sound right about that, but Cooper concentrated on getting the papers signed. "Your signature on these documents will make it harder for them." When Todd still didn't relent, he added, "Wouldn't it feel great to stick it to them?"

He remained silent.

"Do it for Sky. Do it for her kid. Don't let her life be like yours. You're the only one who can stop your parents."

Again complete silence followed his words. The bartender eyed them, and Coop could sense Judd and Walker's restless movements. What did it take to get through to the man?

"Do you have a pen?"

The words came out low, but Cooper heard them. He quickly fished the pen out of the envelope and handed it to him.

"Do you want to read it first?"

"No. I trust you."

Damn. Maybe the man wasn't such a wimp.

"Sign where the red sticky tabs are."

Without another word, Todd Spencer signed away his rights and gave Skylar a boost in keeping Kira.

"Thank you," Cooper said, sliding the papers back into the envelope. "May I ask you another question?"

"You've had your quota." He pierced Cooper with a sharp glance. "Unless you threaten to break my arm again."

"I was desperate," he admitted.

"And effective." Todd drained his glass. "Another Scotch, Joe." He looked at Cooper again, seeming more relaxed. "Another Scotch and I'll probably tell you anything."

Cooper thought it was as good a time as any to get the doubts out of his head. "You said your parents would never let go of the child. What did you mean by that?"

"Ah." He took the drink before Joe could set it on the bar. "Money. Isn't it always about money?"

"I wouldn't know. I've never had enough to worry about it."

"Well." Todd downed a large swallow. "In the Spencer family money is God, and you hold on to it at all costs."

"What does that have to do with Kira?"

Todd shifted to face him. "My dad is an only child and so am I. Grandfather Spencer left an enormous estate. He was pissed at me for not going into the Spencer pharmaceutical company, so I was left a trust fund that will keep me happy for the rest of my life."

"I'm not following you." Todd was drunk and Cooper wasn't sure he knew what he was saying. But Coop kept listening.

"Skylar's kid is a Spencer heir, the only heir, since I've had a vasectomy. That entitles her to a share of the wealth, a very big share. And whoever has custody of her will control the money. That's what Grandfather's will states. That's why my parents want custody. Keep the money in the family and all that."

"That's the reason they've been looking for Sky and wanting a DNA test done?"

"Bingo." Todd slapped the bar with his palm. "Give the man a cigar."

Out of the corner of his eye, Coop saw Walker and Judd getting to their feet.

"Wait a minute." To Cooper it still didn't sound right. "That doesn't make sense. You denied Kira is yours, so if they'd left it alone, no one would have been the wiser."

"Oh, you poor sucker, you do not know my parents." Todd downed more Scotch. "They like to keep their eggs all in one basket, so to speak. Skylar knows the Spencers have money and my parents knew one day she'd figure out that the kid was entitled to something. They wanted to nip that in the bud, even though I repeatedly told them the baby wasn't mine. They're going to make sure Skylar doesn't see a dime of that cash, and they'll stick the kid in boarding school and dole out her inheritance as they wish."

Todd slapped the manila envelope lying on the bar. "These papers aren't worth squat. Their lawyer will chew them up like a pit bull and spit them in your face."

"You're really a heartless bastard."

"Yeah." Todd slid off the stool. "I had real good teachers. And if I know my parents, Mr. Yates, your ass will be back in prison before the night is out." He staggered from the bar.

Cooper felt as if he'd been sucker punched by the gutless wonder of the world. How could Todd Spencer not care about his own child's welfare? But it didn't matter. Todd didn't matter. If Carl Devlin was a pit bull, then Ms. Dunbar was a rottweiler, and Cooper was betting she wouldn't be chewed up so easily.

Todd Spencer occupied his mind on the flight back to Austin. The suave, polished man with an attitude was the type who attracted Red. He was the father of her child. Cooper was nothing like him. He was a cowboy and always would be, just as Everett had once told him. The future Coop envisioned of having his own ranch was now gone.

He shifted uncomfortably and thought about prison, but that didn't matter, either. It was a risk he was willing to take. For Red. For Kira. Red had to keep her daughter. If that meant he had to give them up, then he would do so.

But his heart would never be the same.

COOPER WAITED FOR Ms. Dunbar in a waiting area down the hall from Kira's room. He couldn't go inside in case a reporter was hanging around.

The tip-tap of heels echoed in the hall and he glanced up as the lawyer slid into a chair next to him. Without a word he handed her the papers.

"Todd Spencer signed everything, but he says it's not going to do you any good. Mr. Devlin will make mince-meat of it."

"Oh, Mr. Yates, you're underestimating me."

"I certainly hope so. Sky has to keep Kira."

"Have some faith in my abilities. Once I figure out their angle, Mr. Devlin won't know what hit him."

Coop took a deep breath. "I know what it is."

She pushed her glasses up the bridge of her nose. "What?"

He told her about the money.

"Hot damn, cowboy. When you do a job, you do it. This is the smoking gun. Oh, yeah, this is what I was looking for. I'll get Purvis on it right away."

"Purvis?"

"My P.I."

"Oh."

Judd and Walker strolled in and Cooper got to his feet. "How's Kira?"

"She's sleeping," Judd replied.

"And Sky?"

"She's exhausted, and worried."

Coop's gut tightened.

Ms. Dunbar got to her feet. "I'm going to take care of that. I just need some time. The hearing has been rescheduled to the day after tomorrow, and I have to have all my ducks in a row by then."

"What if Kira isn't out of the hospital?" Cooper asked.

"The show will go on without her."

"That's—"

"Here, look," Judd interrupted. "I took a picture of Kira on my phone so you can see her."

Cooper touched the small screen. "She looks so lost in that bed."

"Her vital signs are better," Walker said. "Much better."

"Cooper Yates."

He looked up to see two police officers standing in the doorway.

This is it.

He sucked in a breath and stepped forward. "That's me."

"You're under arrest for violating your probation. Put your hands behind your back, please." One cop snapped handcuffs on him and a chill shot through Cooper. But he fought all those fears churning inside him, mostly the fear of being locked up again. He closed his eyes and saw Red's blue eyes, and a calm came over him.

"You have the right—"

"Wait a minute, eager beaver." Ms. Dunbar got in the officer's face. "I'm his attorney and I demand—"

"Take it down to the station," the officer replied. "For now he's going to jail." He gave Cooper a nudge toward the door and the trio walked out into the hall. Walker, Judd and Ms. Dunbar were right behind them.

"Hang on, Coop," Walker called. "I'll meet you at the station."

Cooper stopped when he saw Carl Devlin and the Spencers standing at the end of the hall. They'd found a way to get rid of him—for good.

Red came out of Kira's room. She glanced at him and then at the Spencers. His heart contracted at the pain on her pale face.

She started toward him, but Walker and Judd blocked her way.

"What's going on?" she asked, her gaze locking with Cooper's.

"Go back into Kira's room," Walker said. "I'll explain later."

"Don't treat me like a child." She shook off his hand. "They're taking him to jail, aren't they?" She glanced at the Spencers. "Those sons of bitches."

"Let's go," the officer said, and nudged Cooper. The trio walked on.

"No!" Red shouted, and Walker and Judd grabbed her as she started to run after them. "No, they can't do this. No!"

Her words echoed down the hallway and Coop closed his eyes as pain gripped his heart. Tears stung the backs of his eyes. His past was hurting her and there was nothing he could do to stop it. Nothing but endure the torment. Nothing but suffer another scar across his skin. This one went all the way into his heart.

SKY JERKED AWAY from Walker and Judd, her eyes blazing. "Why aren't you doing something to help Cooper?"

"It's out of our hands now," Walker said.

"That's crap. You've been in law enforcement a long time. You can do something."

Walker tipped his hat. "I'm on my way to the station, but don't expect any miracles. Cooper left the county without informing his probation officer."

"Like he had time for that," she retorted. "My daughter's life was in jeopardy. We didn't have time to stop and get permission."

"I'll make that very clear and Ms. Dunbar will do her magic, so please calm down."

She took a long breath, her insides quivering like Jell-O. "Thank you. I'm just…"

Judd put his arm around her. "Walker knows."

"I'll be in touch." Walker strolled down the hall, past the Spencers.

Jonathan, Cybil and their lawyer moved toward her.

"Stay calm," Judd said.

"You might have to hit me with a stun gun for that."

"I'll get Cait."

"Chicken."

Judd squeezed her shoulder as the trio stopped in front of her.

"My clients would like to see their granddaughter," Mr. Devlin said in a voice that burned her skin like heat from an oven. But Sky remained reasonably calm.

"Over my dead body."

"I'll get a court order."

"Knock yourself out."

"You're making this difficult, Ms. Belle."

She took a step closer to him. "It's only just begun, Mr. Devlin, so strap on your gun belt. It's going to be the fight of your life."

CHAPTER FIFTEEN

SKY WALKED INTO THE ROOM seething.

Cait glanced at her and then at Judd. "What happened?"

"They arrested Cooper."

"Damn it! How did they find out?"

"Devlin's done his homework." Judd went to his wife and wrapped an arm around her waist. "The Spencers were here to make sure Coop was taken away. It will make their case stronger."

"I have to see him." Sky paced. "But I can't leave Kira."

"Mommy…" her daughter murmured, and Sky rushed to the bed.

"I'm here, baby." She kissed her cheek.

"I don't feel good."

"I know, precious."

"Hold me."

Sky gathered her child into her arms, careful of the IV. The nurse had taken the oxygen mask off for a while. She picked up Kira's Elmo, which Cait had brought, and sat in the rocker by the bed, cradling her.

"Would you like some ice cream?" She laid Elmo on Kira's stomach and she clutched the toy.

Kira shook her head.

She wasn't eating a thing and Sky was running out of tricks to make her.

"Where's Coo, Mommy?"

Sky bit her lip and searched for an answer. "He's at the ranch. Someone has to take care of the cows." Lying was easy when it came to protecting her baby.

"I want Coo." Her lower lip trembled.

So does Mommy.

Judd squatted in front of them. "I'm going down to the cafeteria to get Mommy and Aunt Cait something to eat. How about an ice-cream sandwich? Georgie likes them."

"'Kay."

"Aunt Cait likes fruit. Would you like some, too?"

"A nana."

"A banana it is."

"Thank you," Sky mouthed as Judd left the room.

Cait sat beside them, stroking Kira's arm. "Aunt Maddie and Gran are coming. Haley and Georgie drew you pictures so we can hang them on the wall. That will be fun."

Kira nodded, her eyes closing. Sky wanted to keep her awake. At least to eat some of the ice cream.

"I love you, precious."

"I love you, too." Kira looked at her with big blue eyes. Both cheeks were bruised and shadows circled her eyes. It was clear her baby had been through a tremendous ordeal. She'd be dead if it hadn't been for Cooper.

Sky's throat closed up and Kira touched her face. "I love Coo, too."

Tears blurred Sky's vision and she was glad when Judd entered the room with a bag. He held out an ice-cream sandwich to Kira.

Sky undid the wrapper and Kira took a bite. Sky

coaxed her to take another, and another, but then she shook her head. The nurse came in with a needle and injected it into the IV.

"She sleeps all the time. I'd like for her to stay awake more," Sky protested.

"The doctor is starting to wean her off the shots. This is the last one for the day. She'll get another before she goes to sleep tonight."

"Good." She stood and laid her baby in the bed, Elmo tucked in one arm. But in other ways it wasn't. Sky would have to deal with questions she wasn't ready to answer.

The nurse left and Maddie and Gran walked in.

"Oh, she's asleep," Gran said, clearly disappointed.

Sky hugged her grandmother. "They just gave her a shot."

"Etta made her favorite chocolate pudding. I thought she might eat it."

Maddie held up a small cooler. "I'll get the nurse to put it in the refrigerator. Maybe she'll eat it later."

"Thanks."

Maddie stopped at the door. "Walker called and told us about Cooper. I was so angry I had to stop on the side of the road and calm down."

"She did," Gran said. "But it didn't help much."

"We're all angry and Kira's asking for him. I don't know what to do." Sky's voice broke. She thought she had everything under control, but she was so afraid.

Her sisters and Gran hugged her, and she gratefully absorbed their love and their support.

"I'll put this in the fridge," Maddie said again. "I'll be right back and we'll talk."

Sky wiped away a tear. "What's in the bag, Gran?" She had a large shopping bag hooked over her forearm.

"Oh." Her grandmother set the bag on the floor. "I brought hats so Kira and I can play movie stars. And pictures Haley and Georgie drew. Little Val, too. Maddie held her hand and let her scribble. When Kira wakes up, we'll hang them somewhere so she can see them."

"She'll like that."

Maddie rushed back in.

"Did Walker tell you anything?" Sky asked.

"He was at the station and the police were booking Cooper. He said Ms. Dunbar was giving them holy hell."

"They're locking him up." Her voice came out faint and hoarse.

"Yes," Maddie replied.

"I have to see Cooper." Sky paced again. "But I don't know how."

"They just gave her a shot," Cait said. "She'll sleep for at least two to three hours. You have time to get there and back, so go. Judd will take you and we'll be here with Kira."

She hesitated.

"Go," Maddie urged.

"I…" Sky glanced at her sleeping child. Kira needed Cooper. She grabbed her purse, which Cait had brought along with her cell charger and a change of clothes. "Let's go, Judd."

COOPER SETTLED INTO a cell with two other inmates. It was dirty, damp and smelled of sweat and urine. The toilet was in the open and foul odors clung like a heavy cloud.

He scooted back on the bare, filthy mattress and stared through the bars at nothing but more cells. No sky. No Red. No freedom.

He had reached the bowels of hell once again.

His gut burned when he thought of Red losing Kira. He'd spend the rest of his life in here to keep that from happening.

"I'm Clyde," an inmate said. "And this is Arnold."

The good ol' boys network from hell.

"I prefer silence." He'd played this game before and knew strength was his only weapon.

"Now that's not… Wait a minute, you're that fellow we saw on TV in the rec room. You pulled a kid out of a well or something."

"Did you not hear me the first time?" Coop moved forward and placed his inmate-issued sneakers flat on the stained concrete floor. Flexing his fists, he stared at the two men.

"Sure, man, sure." They moved away to their own bunks.

He let out a breath and felt the sting in his hands. After booking him, a nurse had checked his wounds and applied antibiotic ointment. But they didn't hurt as bad as the pain in his heart.

"Yates," a guard called.

Cooper stood and walked to the cell door.

"You have a visitor."

"Who?"

He looked at his clipboard. "Skylar Belle."

"No. I'm not seeing anyone. I didn't put anyone on my visitor's list." He didn't want her in this awful place. He didn't want her to see him in his inmate garb. "Tell her to take care of her daughter and forget about me."

The guard inclined his head and walked away, the keys on his belt jangling.

It was over for Coop and Red. Truly over. It should

never have begun. He'd poisoned her life and he'd regret that for the rest of his.

Tears stung the backs of his eyes and he plopped onto the mattress. He hadn't cried in years, and he wouldn't now. He was doing the right thing.

Besides, if he cried it would blow his tough stance to hell with these yahoos.

But he wanted to. God, he wanted to.

"I'M SORRY, MA'AM. He refuses to see you."

"That can't be true," Sky said. "He's just being honorable. That's the way he is."

"Still. It's his choice."

She turned to Walker, who had joined them. "Do something. I have to see him."

"He thinks he's doing the right thing for you and Kira."

"He's not."

"Give him some time."

"I don't have time." She dug for her wallet in her purse. Flipping it open, she found a photo of herself and Kira. On the back, Sky scribbled a message.

She handed it to the guard. "Could you please give this to him?"

"Ma'am."

"It's just a photo," Walker said. "What could it hurt?"

"This isn't a hotel, you know, and he has rights."

"As one lawman to another, please."

"Oh, all right." The guard snatched the picture from her hand and walked away.

"We better go," Judd said.

"Let's wait, just for a minute," Sky pleaded. "He might change his mind."

"God, you Belle women are stubborn."

"And you love us." Sky pinched his cheek.

"Yeah. One more than the others."

"Yates," the guard called.

Cooper rolled to his feet. Now what?

"The lady wanted you to have this." He poked a photo through the bars.

Cooper took it and stared down at the two curly-haired redheads, both smiling. Both breaking his heart. To stop seeing their faces, he turned it over. Something was written on the back: "We love you."

His breath left his lungs and he had trouble breathing. Sky was pulling out all the stops, but he couldn't waver in his decision.

"Guard," he shouted.

"What?" The man stomped back, clearly irritated.

"I'll see her."

"Like I told the lady, this isn't a hotel and I'm not at your beck and call."

"It won't take long. Five minutes tops."

The guy rubbed his chin. "Mmm. Since you pulled her kid out of a well, I'll allow it. Five minutes."

The guard unlocked the cell and took Coop's arm. They went down a long hall and then another. From there he was shown into a cubicle. A partition separated him from his visitor, with a phone available so he could talk to her.

"Sit. She'll be here shortly. I'm watching you."

The door on the left opened and Red rushed in, her red curls everywhere. She looked so beautiful. And tired.

She took a seat and touched the Plexiglas with one hand. He wanted to press his hand against hers, but resisted.

Reaching for the phone, he motioned for her to pick up hers. "You shouldn't be here."

"You shouldn't be in this place."

"But I am. That's my life. I knew the risk and I gladly took it. Concentrate on Kira. Not on me."

"I can't do that."

"If you want to keep Kira, you have to."

"She's asking for you and I don't know what to tell her."

He swallowed hard. "You'll think of something." He swallowed again. "Rufus can run High Five. You might have to hire some help, but—"

"No." She shook her head, her curls bouncing. "High Five can't survive without you. I can't survive without you."

"Forget about me, Red."

The blue of her eyes turned to fire. "I'm a Belle and we fight for what we want. I'm not stopping until these ridiculous charges are dropped."

"Listen to me. Kira's life is in the balance here. Todd signed away his rights, so put all you energies into fighting for her. You and I are over. We should never have gotten involved in the first place." He pushed back his chair. "Goodbye, Red."

"It's not goodbye. Cooper. Cooper!" He heard the screams coming from the phone, but didn't look back. He knocked on the door and the guard let him out. Clutching the photo in his hand, he walked to his cell. He'd meant to give it back, but he wasn't that strong.

SKY SLAMMED DOWN the phone. "It's not over, Cooper Yates. It's *not* over. It's…" Try as she might, she couldn't stop the tears that burst from her eyes.

Judd touched her arm. "Sky."

She wiped her cheeks with the back of her hand.

"Let's return to the hospital."

"I'll never give up, Judd. Never."

"I know."

The ride was made in silence. Sky was drained, but her fight had only begun.

In Kira's room, she saw her daughter was still asleep. She kissed her and sat down, then stood again. Sky had so many turbulent thoughts, so much restless energy.

"Sky, please sit down," Cait begged. "You can't keep this up."

"There has to be a way out." She started to pace. "I don't know how, though. I just want to snatch Kira and disappear into a foreign country. But I can't leave Cooper behind." She looked at her sisters. Judd and Walker were in the hall and Gran was half-asleep in a chair. "Would you like to help me with a jailbreak?"

"I'm asking the nurse to give you something," Maddie said. "You're sleep deprived and losing your mind."

"I'm losing everything," Sky cried.

Cait and Maddie shared a glance.

"Don't do that. I hate it when you do that."

Cait and Maddie grabbed her arms and pushed her into a chair. "Take a deep breath," Maddie said. "And another."

"It's going to take a whole lot of bitchy, some bossiness and a double dose of Maddie's goodness to get out of this situation. Now think," Cait ordered. "And rationally, for heaven's sake. We're not breaking anyone out of jail."

And just like that the despair and panic vanished. She could hear her father's voice so clearly.

Sometimes you have to stand and fight for what you

want. It won't be easy, but you're a Belle and you can do it.

Yes, she could.

She rose to her feet. "I know what I have to do."

Cait and Maddie shared another glance. "Is it legal?" Cait asked.

"Mommy," Kira mumbled, and Sky rushed to the bed.

"I'm here, precious." She kissed her, and Kira began to sob, loudly.

Sky gathered her close, stroking her hair. "It's okay. Mommy's here."

"Georgie said to tell you hi," Maddie said, trying to distract her. "He'll come see you when he can."

Kira peeped out from Sky's arms. "Why can't he come see me now?"

"Because you're in the hospital, baby."

"Why am I in the hospital?"

Sky swallowed. "Don't you remember?"

"Uh-uh."

Sky figured the truth was the best medicine. "You wanted to go outside, but I wouldn't let you because I wanted you to rest your knee."

"And I pulled a chair to the front door and used Etta's broom to unlock it."

She was remembering, but Sky didn't know if she wanted her to remember everything. She didn't want her to suppress it, either.

"Why did you do that when Mommy told you no?"

"I saw the dogs and they wanted me to play with them. I ran around the house and crawled under the fence. I called and Boots came and I chased him and..."

"And what?"

Kira looked up at her. "Did I fall down?"

"Yes, baby, you fell down."

"That's all I 'member."

Thank God. Sky gripped her child.

"I was bad." More loud crying followed the statement.

Sky rocked her. "Shh. Shh. You're not bad. I love you."

The sobbing woke Gran and she came to the bed. "What's wrong with my baby?"

"Gran," Kira wailed, and held out her arms. But the IV kept her immobile. "I can't hug Gran. Take it out, Mommy. Take it out."

Sky held a finger in Kira's face. "Calm down."

Cait pushed the nurse's button and Gran stepped closer. Leaning over, she kissed her great-granddaughter. "Don't cry, my baby."

The nurse came in and Cait asked, "Do you know when she can get the IV out?"

"When she starts eating and drinking. That's the doctor's orders."

"Do you hear that, big shot?"

Sky was glad Cait had taken over, because Kira probably wouldn't do it for her. She'd cling and beg instead.

Kira nodded.

"So what's it going to be? Are you going to eat and drink?"

She nodded again.

"If you don't, we'll have to put it back in," the nurse said.

"I will," Kira promised, and the nurse had it removed in minutes.

Applying tape where the IV had been, she asked, "Now what can I get you to eat?"

"Bacon and eggs. That's what Coo eats."

The nurse smiled. "What kind of juice?"

"Apple," Kira shouted.

"I'll order it," she stated, and walked out.

Gran scooped up Kira and sat with her in the rocking chair. Sky stared at the bruises on her daughter's body and her heart twisted in pain. Her knee was severely swollen, as was her elbow. Rope burns were visible on her ankles, and black-and-blue spots dotted her skin. But Sky knew Kira was lucky to be alive.

Gran pointed to the bag on the floor and Sky took it to her.

"Look what I brought," the older woman said, pulling out the hats.

"Oh, boy, Gran. Who we gonna be?"

"Well, I think you shall be the beautiful Elizabeth Taylor." Gran placed a hat of the forties with yellow and red flowers and ribbons on Kira's head. "And I shall be the elegant Katharine Hepburn." She plopped the other hat on hers.

Maddie slipped an arm through Sky's. "Kira's getting better."

"Yes. But it's hard to see her hurt so badly."

Maddie rubbed Sky's forearm. "We're right here if you need us."

The nurse brought a tray in and Kira sat in a chair to eat, with the hat on her head. To Sky's surprise, she actually ate, and drank the juice.

"I'll go get the pudding," Maddie said. "Maybe she'll eat it."

"Thanks."

"Mommy." Kira looked at her. "I'm eating."

"I'm so proud."

Kira then glanced at Gran. "Does Elizabeth Taylor eat bacon and eggs?"

"Oh, most definitely," she replied.

Maddie came back with the pudding and she, Cait and Gran hovered around the little girl. Sky thought this would be a good time to do what she had to.

"Precious, Mommy's going into the hall to make a phone call."

Kira's blue eyes swung to her. "Are you coming back?" A slight quaver entered her voice.

"Baby, Mommy always comes back."

"Yeah." She dived into the pudding, and Sky stepped into the hall and walked down to the small waiting room.

She poked out a number and waited. Finally, the phone clicked on.

"Mother, it's Sky. I need your help."

"If you're calling me Mother, it has to be bad." Sky usually called her mom by her given name.

"It is. Kira has had an accident."

"Oh my God. What happened?"

Sky told her everything about the well, the Spencers and Cooper.

"Cooper Yates works on High Five?"

"Yes."

"How ironic is that?"

"He was born in High Cotton."

"Well, I'll be damned. It's a small world."

"Mother…"

"How's Kira?"

"She's getting better, but she's severely bruised."

"I'll catch the next flight. Where are you?"

Sky told her. "First, I need a favor, and, Mother, I need you to keep this one."

"God, when you call me Mother in that tone of voice, guilt slams into my chest. I wasn't the perfect mother, but I did my best."

"Please help me."

"What do you need?"

"I know you're not on speaking terms with Everett."

"Hell, no. He's in prison."

Sky took a breath. "I want Cooper cleared of the assault charge. You can get Everett to drop the charges."

"Sugar, that's a done deal. I don't think you can retry a case. And I'd rather curl up to a rattlesnake than Everett."

"Mother, I know you can do something. I want Cooper's record cleared. He's suffered unjustly long enough. Kira and I need him."

"You're asking for a miracle, and it's not going to happen. I mean, what's the worst-case scenario? They'll extend his probation or…"

"Or send him back to prison. Please, Mother."

"Sugar, you're not being rational. Besides, I'm in Florida with Richard, visiting his son, and he's not going to be pleased if I leave. I know he's going to ask me to marry him, and even though his kids grate on my nerves, I'm going to accept. I can't wait for you to meet him."

Sky stood, blood shooting through her veins in anger. "I do not care about Richard, his family or your impending marriage. My concern is keeping my daughter and setting Cooper free. If you don't help me, you're out of our lives for good. Understand?"

"Yes, Skylar. I understand perfectly."

Sky sagged under the weight of her emotions. "Please, help us."

"I'll do what I can."

Sky clicked off. *I love you* echoed through her mind,

but she and Julia never had that kind of loving relationship. At times, Sky thought she hated her. But she didn't. And she prayed Julia would not let her down as she had so many times in the past.

CHAPTER SIXTEEN

KIRA CONTINUED TO IMPROVE and Sky was able to get some rest on the cot in the room. She asked the nurse not to administer the sedative, and Kira went to sleep on her own, tired out from playing with Gran and her aunts.

When Kira woke up in the night, the nurse gave her something for pain, and she went back to sleep. She was still sleeping when the doctor came in, and Sky had a chance to talk to her.

"The hearing is tomorrow and I can't leave Kira here."

Dr. Morgan sat in a chair, the chart on her lap. "She's doing very well and I see no reason you can't take her home tomorrow."

"Really?"

"Yes. She just has to take life quieter for a couple of weeks or so. I'll give you a stronger pain med and a sedative if you need it."

"I…"

"I know you don't want to give her a lot of medication."

"No. I want her to be as normal as possible."

"I'll try my best to keep her that way." The doctor pushed back her blond hair in a nervous gesture. "Carl Devlin contacted me."

"What?" Sky sat up straight.

"He wanted me to testify on the Spencers' behalf."

Sky swallowed. "Did you agree?"

"Hell, no. I've already told Ms. Dunbar I'd testify for you."

"Oh, thank you." The weight on her chest eased.

"Of course, I'm booked solid tomorrow, but Ms. Dunbar is getting my testimony today. She's one go-getter."

"She is." Sky wondered why she hadn't seen the colorful lawyer recently. Hopefully, she was putting a killer case together.

Dr. Morgan stood. "I'll have Kira's release papers ready early in the morning."

"Thank you. Thank you for everything."

"Good luck tomorrow."

"Dr. Morgan," Sky called before she could leave. "May I give Kira a bath?"

"Yes. I was going to mention that. Warm baths will help her joints and help to calm her. There's a big tub down the hall. I'll send the nurse in. Again, good luck."

"Thank you."

Kira loved the water and Sky let her play in it as long as she wanted. Sky even scrubbed all the dirt out of her hair, then wrapped her in a big white towel and carried her back to the room.

Cait, Judd and Gran came in the afternoon and the light was back in her daughter's eyes. Kira was going to be fine.

Or was she?

Tomorrow loomed closer and closer. The urge to run was strong, but Cooper and her dad said Sky had to fight. But it wasn't easy. Not with her daughter's future hanging in the balance.

Ms. Dunbar arrived and Sky met her in the waiting room, while Cait and Gran took care of Kira. The lawyer balanced papers on her lap. "Are you ready for tomorrow, hon?"

"No. I'm worried out of my mind."

"And you want to run."

Sky jerked her head around. "How do you know that?"

"It's your pattern. From the first moment you knew the Spencers wanted custody, you ran, and you've been running ever since. Well, it's time to stop and put on your boxing gloves, because it's going to be a fight."

"I keep telling myself that."

"Keep doing it."

"What are my chances?"

Ms. Dunbar pushed her glasses up the bridge of her nose. "It's up to the judge to decide if the Spencers have just cause to remove Kira from your care. He will rule in the best interest of the child, and I'm going to do my damnedest to pull on his heartstrings. Now—" she shuffled through the papers "—let's go over a few things. I have Todd's release of parental rights. That's in our favor. I just got Dr. Morgan's testimony and she gave you a glowing report. Kira's doctors in Tennessee and in Kentucky also faxed stellar testimonies of your capabilities as a mother. All in our favor."

Sky felt much better as Ms. Dunbar flipped through more papers. "Now the inheritance."

"What inheritance?"

The lawyer looked over the rim of her glasses. "Didn't the cowboy tell you?"

"No. I haven't had a chance to really talk to him."

"Kira Belle is the sole heir of the Spencer fortune."

"What? How do you know that?"

"The cowboy kept pressing for a reason Todd's parents wanted the child so badly, and that's what he was told."

"This is about money?" Anger replaced the worry.

"Yep. Lots of money."

"How much?"

"Millions."

Sky gasped. "But Todd could have other children."

"He's had a vasectomy. Kira's the only heir."

"So it's not about Kira. It's about the money?"

"They go hand in hand, hon. Whoever has custody of Kira will control the money."

"I don't want the damn money. I just want to keep my child."

"Think about that, hon. The money will allow Kira to have the best medical care available."

Sky remained determined. "I don't want their money. I can take care of my own kid."

"Good Lord, you're stubborn."

"I just want the Spencers out of our lives."

"I'll do my best." Ms. Dunbar stuck the papers back in her briefcase. "Dr. Morgan says she's releasing Kira in the morning."

"Yes. I can't leave here without her."

"What will you do with her during the hearing?"

"My sisters will take care of her. This won't take long, will it?"

"No, but I suggest you have your sisters keep Kira away from the courthouse."

"Why?"

"Because if the judge doesn't see things our way, then it's time to run."

"What?"

"I'll get you and Kira out of Texas and in a secret hiding place where the Spencers will never find you. No way are we turning over that child."

"But—but..." Sky spluttered, caught completely off guard.

"I'm a confident lawyer, but this time I'm covering all my bases. Just be prepared."

Sky stiffened her shoulders, remembering how Cooper had told her to fight. "I'm not running and I'm not losing my child. Cooper wants me to fight and that's what I'll do."

"Hot damn. I think we have a winner." Ms. Dunbar stood. "Keep that confidence going."

Sky frowned. "Are you testing me?"

"I want you to walk into that courtroom with no doubt in your mind. I want you to walk in—period. A no-show is not an option."

"Oh."

Ms. Dunbar slung her purse strap over her shoulder. "I managed to get Mr. Yates's hearing on the docket at one tomorrow. They've already transported him back to Giddings."

"How did you do that so quickly?"

"I pulled some strings, made some threats, bullshit stuff that gets results. I know you both want this over with as soon as possible."

"Yes."

"I'll see you at ten in the morning, and keep thinking positive thoughts."

That was hard to do. Sky wavered from panic to hysteria and then back to panic. The only bright spot was Kira's excitement in going home. She wanted to see

Coo. Sky told her he would be busy working away from the ranch. God, she hated lying, but she was praying Cooper would be home by the end of the day.

Before going to bed, Sky called Julia. They had a bad connection, but she made sure her mother knew the hearing times and the location.

Sky had an uneasy feeling as she curled up on the cot. Julia sounded distant. Was she even trying to help? Or was she was so wrapped up in Richard what's-his-name that once again she'd forgotten her daughter?

As she drifted into sleep, she prayed for a miracle.

And she prayed for Cooper's touch.

THE NEXT MORNING WAS RUSHED. Cait and Judd arrived at the hospital before six and they were on the road heading home by seven.

Maddie, Walker and the kids were waiting for them at High Five, along with Gran, Etta and Rufus. Judd carried Kira in, and her eyes grew big as she saw all the balloons and streamers. Maddie's work, for sure. Etta had made a welcome-home cake. Judd carried Kira to the kitchen so she could see.

"He's going to make such a wonderful father." Cait sighed.

Judd stood Kira on her feet and she "oohed" and "aahed" over the cake, her eyes large in her pale face.

Sky held her hand as she limped into the parlor. Blankets and pillows were piled on the sofa and Kira curled up in them. Gran sat by her, stroking her legs.

Georgie ran forward and Sky held her breath, but he hugged Kira gently. "I missed you."

"I missed you, too."

Maddie was snapping pictures holding Val in one arm.

"We brought all kinds of games. Wanna play?"

"Kira has to be quiet," Maddie reminded him.

"Can we watch a movie?"

"Yes, you may, sweet son."

"It's time," Walker said.

Sky knelt by the sofa. "Mommy has to go into town for a little while." Her voice broke and she gathered Kira in her arms. "I love you."

"I love you, too, Mommy, and I won't be bad. I'll be good."

"Thank you. I'll be back as soon as I can."

"Will Coo be with you?"

She bit her lip and found it hard to lie. "I'll do my best."

"'Kay."

Sky walked away before she burst into tears. She had to remain positive. Maddie handed Walker the baby and followed her to the door.

"I'll take very good care of her."

Sky reached in her purse for Kira's meds. "Give her one dose in two hours." She held up another bottle. "If she starts to cry and says she doesn't feel good, give her a teaspoon of this."

Maddie took the bottles and then hugged her. "Walker will be right behind you, and he has orders to call as soon as the judge rules."

Sky ran to the car, where Judd and Cait were waiting. They didn't say much on the way into Giddings. The strain was getting to all of them. She tried her mother several times, but Julia wasn't answering. That hurt, but Sky walked into the courtroom with confidence, and intended to walk out with it, too.

She eased into a chair next to Ms. Dunbar. Cait, Judd

and Walker took seats behind them, with the Spencers and Mr. Devlin to their left.

"The Honorable Judge Harmon Willet." The bailiff announced the judge's arrival, and the show started.

"Ready, hon?" Ms. Dunbar asked.

"Yes." And she was. She was ready to get this over with so she could help Cooper. But her heart was about to pound out of her chest.

"Remember the burden is on them. Mr. Devlin has to prove just cause to remove Kira from your care."

And the other lawyer set out to do just that. He painted her as a party girl out for a good time, who got pregnant because she was too drunk to think of protection. He painted her as an unfit mother who dragged her daughter from state to state when the child needed a stable environment to deal with a crippling disease. And then he painted her as a mother who endangered the life of her child by not watching her and caring for her as she should. He topped it off with Sky having an affair with an ex-con, right in front of her daughter. He backed everything up with documentation, just as Sky knew he would. Her worst nightmare had come true.

Sky curled her hands into fists and held on to her temper, which was being shredded to pieces.

Mr. Devlin ended his speech by saying, "Jonathan and Cybil Spencer are very concerned about Ms. Belle's lifestyle and the company she keeps. They are doubly concerned about their granddaughter's welfare. Kira Belle could have easily lost her life by falling into an old well shaft because Ms. Belle wasn't watching her properly. My clients offer their granddaughter two loving grandparents who will always be there for her and care for all her needs, making sure she receives the best

medical attention possible." Mr. Devlin took a breath.
"Your Honor, I respectfully request that the child, Kira
Belle, be placed with the Spencers."

Ms. Dunbar grabbed a stack of papers at least ten
inches deep and carried them to the judge, plopping
them in front of him.

"What is this, Ms. Dunbar?" he asked, irritation in his
voice.

"Evidence to refute everything Mr. Devlin has just
said."

"This is a hearing. Could you please give me a short
version?"

"Yes, Your Honor." Ms. Dunbar held up one finger.
"First of all, bringing up Ms. Belle's college days is a
low blow. I'm a different woman than I was in college.
So is Ms. Belle. And I'm sure you are, too, Judge."

"Stick to the case."

She smiled slightly. "Second, Ms. Belle moved her
daughter from state to state because she was hiding from
the Spencers. They wanted to take her child and, as any
good mother would, she made sure that didn't happen."
Ms. Dunbar pointed to the papers. "The sheets with blue
tabs are testimonies from doctors and nurses she saw
along the way, doctors who took care of her daughter.
There's also a testimony from Dr. Jana Morgan, who has
been Kira's doctor since Ms. Belle brought her back to
Texas. The green tabs are testimonies from the people
of High Cotton, her neighbors who daily see her inter-
action with and concern for her child. They're all
glowing reports of Ms. Belle's care of her daughter, her
capabilities as a mother."

Ms. Dunbar took a breath. "Third, the accident and
Cooper Yates. Kira was a having a bad spell with her

knee, so Ms. Belle was keeping her in. Kira was feeling better and wanted to go outside and play. Ms. Belle said no, and stayed home from work to be there for her daughter. While Ms. Belle was on the phone, Kira found a way to get out of the house. In a split second she was gone, looking for the ranch's dogs. Kira is an impetuous and ingenious child. If we held parents accountable for that, we'd have a lot of moms and dads in jail."

Ms. Dunbar walked back to the table. "Now, about Cooper Yates…"

"This hearing isn't about Cooper Yates, Ms. Dunbar. Move on."

"I just want it noted he was the one who devised a plan to pull Kira out of the well."

"I've seen it on the news, Ms. Dunbar. This is a hearing about custody of Kira Belle. Do you have anything else?"

"You bet I do." She picked up a manila folder from the desk and carried it to the judge. "Todd Spencer, Kira's biological father, released his parental rights. And he also stated who he thought would be best to raise his child."

Mr. Devlin stood and buttoned his jacket. "May I see that, Your Honor?"

"By all means." He handed it to him.

The lawyer read through it and placed it in front of the judge, his expression closed.

"And, Your Honor," Ms. Dunbar continued, "after a lot of digging and research, I've found that Kira Belle is the sole heir to the Spencer fortune and the only reason her grandparents are here today seeking custody. The papers with the red tabs contain all the information I've collected."

Mr. Devlin was on his feet. "That's total nonsense. Ms. Dunbar is trying to pull a rabbit out of a hat."

"I'm just beginning—"

The judge held up a hand, stopping them. "I've heard enough." He picked up the stack of papers and stood. "I'll have my ruling in thirty minutes."

"What happened?" Sky asked. "Why wouldn't he listen to what you had to say?"

"Because these small-town judges are sticklers for procedure. Damn it! *Damn* it!"

"What does it mean?" Sky's breath lodged in her throat and she had trouble breathing. Was it time to run? No. She would not. But it took every ounce of courage she had to stay rooted to the spot.

Cait grasped her arm. "Let's go outside and take a breather."

In the entry, they sat on a bench. "They can't take my child. They can't."

Cait hugged her. "They won't. Judge Willet is not senile."

Sky wiped away a tear. "I wish Cooper was here. I need him."

"I'm sure he's thinking about you."

Sky ran her fingers through her curls. "Dad said that one day I'd have to grow up, but this is a nightmare."

They didn't say anything after that. Sky held on to her sister for support and prayed for a miracle.

Too soon Judd poked his head out the door. "He's coming back."

Sky stood, refusing to lose her confidence, and went back inside.

"This is it, hon," Ms. Dunbar said. "Just stay composed."

She didn't know how to do that when someone was about to rip out her heart. Her palms were sweaty and her insides rolled with a sick feeling. No. She would remain strong. For Kira. And for Cooper.

The judge took his seat, signed some papers to his left and typed something into his laptop. He didn't even acknowledge their presence. Finally, he folded his hands and looked at them.

Ms. Dunbar squeezed Sky's clenched, shaking hands.

"I've read through the testimonies of the doctors, nurses and the people of High Cotton who have known Ms. Belle personally and have witnessed her care and love for her child." His gaze swung to the Spencers. "Mr. Devlin, you haven't shown just cause to remove Kira Belle from her mother. Your petition is denied."

OhmyGod! OhmyGod! Thank you! Tears welled in Sky's eyes and she trembled, but joy suffused her whole body.

They would *not* take her child.

"Your Honor." The Spencers' lawyer was on his feet.

"Mr. Devlin, I also glanced at Ms. Dunbar's research on the Spencer estate. Whatever monies Kira Belle is entitled to, I hope you see that she receives them. I strongly suggest you work out the details with Ms. Dunbar. This case is adjourned."

The judge pounded the gavel and Sky jumped up and hugged Ms. Dunbar and then Cait. Walker was already on the phone with Maddie.

"WHAT DO YOU WANT to do?" Carl Devlin stuffed papers into his briefcase.

"What options do we have?" Jonathan asked.

"Try again for custody at a later date or make a settlement with Skylar Belle."

"We're not giving her any money," Cybil declared.

"That's not an option, I'm afraid. Jon Spencer's will states clearly what an heir is to receive, and as you know, it's enormous."

"How do we avoid this and get Skylar's fingers out of the Spencer estate?" Jonathan glanced to where the Belles were standing.

"I suggest a onetime life settlement. That way the child won't have shares in the company or a seat on the board, nor will she be entitled to any of the profits in the years ahead."

"Work it out," Jonathan said.

"Ms. Dunbar is not going to accept any measly offer. She's done her homework."

"Start low and make a deal so we can get out of this horrid town."

Carl picked up his briefcase. "Do you want the right to see the child?"

Jonathan glanced at his wife, and then turned back to the lawyer. "No. Make it final."

CAIT NUDGED SKY with an elbow and out of the corner of her eye she saw Mr. Devlin and the Spencers walk over.

"We need to talk," the lawyer said to Ms. Dunbar.

She glanced at her watch. "I have another court hearing in less than an hour. It will have to be tomorrow. Ten o'clock. My office."

"My clients are ready to make a deal today."

Ms. Dunbar wiped a speck from his lapel and he frowned at her audacity. "I'll be making the deals and it will be tomorrow." She took Sky's arm and led her from the courtroom.

"I don't want their money," Sky said in the hall.

"Stuff that pride where I don't see it," Ms. Dunbar replied. "You daughter deserves it and I'm going to make sure she receives every dime she has coming to her."

"She's right, Sky," Cait said. "Do it for Kira. She might need it as she grows older."

Sky closed her eyes briefly. "I don't want anything from them. I don't want to be beholden to them. I don't want them in Kira's life."

"Well, hon, I don't think they'll have a problem with that. I'll have the money sent to a bank in Giddings, with you as executor. It will be in a trust for Kira whenever she needs it. I suspect it will be a lump sum payment and you won't ever have to see them again. How does that sound?"

"Like you're a miracle worker." Sky managed a smile.

"Didn't I tell you?" She glanced at her watch. "I've got to run. I want to speak to the cowboy before the hearing."

"Please tell him about Kira and…that we love him."

"That will be the first thing I tell him." Ms. Dunbar walked off, briefcase in hand, her heels tap-tapping.

Since Cooper's hearing was in the same district court-room across from the courthouse, they waited just outside. Sky looked around the hallway.

"Are you looking for Cooper?" Cait asked.

"No. They won't let me see him. I'm looking for my mother. She was supposed to be here." Sky sank onto a bench. "She's not coming. She let me down once again."

"Sky…"

"It's okay. I don't know why I thought she could help in the first place. I was grasping at straws."

She reached for her cell and called to check on Kira.

Maddie said she was sleeping. They talked about the good news for a minute and then Sky clicked off.

She had her daughter. Thank God that angst was over. But would she have Cooper?

CHAPTER SEVENTEEN

COOPER SAT IN A ROOM in his regular clothes, waiting for his lawyer. He knew the hearing was at ten and it should be over. What had happened? He jammed both hands through his hair. Did they take Kira from Red? He had to know. Where in the hell was Ms. Dunbar?

She breezed in, all smiles, and his heart lifted. This had to be good.

"How did it go?"

"We won. Skylar gets to keep her daughter."

"Oh, thank God. So it's over?"

"Not quite, cowboy. Now we have to work some magic on your case."

"I'm not worried about myself. I just wanted Sky and Kira to stay together."

A guard opened the door and handcuffed him to take him to the courthouse. But Coop knew he could handle whatever this day brought. Red and Kira were safe.

Ms. Dunbar followed the squad car to the district court, where she demanded the cuffs be removed. The officer complied. The lawyer knew how to get results.

"Stiff upper lip, cowboy," she said. "I'll tell you the same thing I told Skylar. Walk into that courtroom with confidence. You did nothing wrong. Got it?"

"Got it."

"In case you need an extra incentive, Skylar said to tell you that she and Kira love you."

"Thanks." His heart felt heavy, though. If this day went bad, he had to disappear out of their lives for good. He didn't want them coming to the prison. He didn't want them near that world.

"Let's go," Ms. Dunbar said, and they followed a guard through a door into the small courtroom.

Cooper stopped short and blinked. The room was packed with the people of High Cotton. What were they doing here?

The Belle family, along with Rufus and Chance, sat in the first row. Coop's eyes zeroed in on Red. Her expression was clouded, worried. His chest expanded with gut-wrenching emotions and he looked away.

He took his seat by Ms. Dunbar.

"All rise for the Honorable Harmon Willet," the bailiff called.

A shuffling noise echoed through the room as people stood and the judge walked to his seat. Everyone resumed theirs.

An assistant D.A. presented the charges and then Ms. Dunbar stood. "Your Honor, this is a waste of taxpayers' money. Mr. Yates has committed no crime. Yes, he left the county without notifying his probation officer, but there were extenuating circumstances."

"I'm well aware of what happened, Ms. Dunbar. It's been all over the news."

"Then you can understand that Mr. Yates did what any normal human being would have done. He took care of the child first, making sure she and her mother were okay."

"Ms. Dunbar, Mr. Yates made a conscious choice

when he got into that ambulance. He could have called his probation officer, but he did nothing."

"Are you serious?"

Cooper glanced at his attorney and had a feeling the cool lady was about to lose it.

"Yeah, Judge." Joe Bob got to his feet. "I was there. The little girl was in bad shape. There wasn't time."

"I was there, too." Charlie stood. "We didn't know what to do, but he did."

"I was there, too," Skully said.

"Me, too," chorused other voices around the courtroom.

The judge banged his gavel three times. "Sit down or I'll have this courtroom cleared."

An uneasy quiet settled in the room.

"I sympathize with everyone, and I'd be inclined to relent in this case. But—" the judge picked up a piece of paper "—the D.A. has been informed of Mr. Yates's activities on the night in question. He flew from Austin to Dallas without informing anyone, though he had time to do so. I'd say ample time to abide by his probation, but he chose not to. That's a blatant disrespect of the law."

"Shit!" Ms. Dunbar said under her breath, but she got to her feet. "Your Honor, I'd like to explain—"

"It's too late, Ms. Dunbar. There are laws for a reason. Mr. Yates violated his probation and he has to face the consequences of that action. I'm prepared to make my ruling. Mr. Yates, please stand."

Cooper stood, his insides coiled into a knot. The quiet intensified. No one moved or made a sound.

"May I say something, Your Honor?" Sky got to her feet and the knot tightened. Coop didn't want her to do this. He didn't want her to grovel for him.

"Ms. Belle, please sit down."

"I will not until…"

Suddenly the click-clack of high heels echoed through the room. The double doors opened and a woman waltzed in, wearing a short, strapless flowered sundress, her red hair hanging down around her bare shoulders.

Red's mother! Julia!

Oh, God! He didn't need that woman here, reminding him of his past. And Everett.

Julia walked up to the judge with a manila envelope in her hand.

He heard a gasp from Red, and Ms. Dunbar whispered, "Who is that?"

"Skylar's mother."

"What's she doing here? No one interrupts a hearing."

From his association with Julia, Coop knew the woman did whatever she pleased.

"Good afternoon, Your Honor." Julia flipped back her long hair. "This Texas heat is a killer."

"Ma'am, what are you doing in my courtroom? If you don't leave, I'll have you arrested."

"Now, Judgie." Julia flashed him a smile and leaned slightly so the judge had a good view of her cleavage. "That's not nice."

The stern official broke out in a sweat. "Ma'am…"

"Oh, please, call me Julia." She ran a hand under her hair and tossed it back in a provocative gesture.

"What…what are you doing in my courtroom?"

"Oh, silly me." She held a hand to her breast. "I almost forgot. I'm here on behalf of Cooper Yates."

What? Had she come to bury him?

"This is a hearing and you're interrupting."

"Oh, posh." Julia waved a hand, the light catching the glint of her diamond rings. "I'm not just anybody. I have information for you." She placed the envelope in front of the judge.

"This is highly irregular."

"What's life without a little irregularity, Judgie?"

A rumble of laughter followed her words. Willet frowned and silence quickly ensued.

The judge pulled papers from the envelope and glanced at them. "Where did you get this?"

"I'm betting you can read." Julia flashed another smile. "It's all legal. Now I think it's time to make your ruling."

"Ma'am, please have a seat."

"Oh, posh. Get this over with."

Sky wanted to sink through the floor, but this was pure Julia. She had the judge wrapped around her finger and she was reeling him in. So many times Sky had seen her mother do this, and she had to wonder what was in the papers. But all she could think was that *her mother hadn't let her down*.

Hadn't let *them* down.

"Mr. Yates, please…" The judge glanced up, straightened his glasses with a confused look. "Oh, you're still standing."

"Yes, Your Honor." Ms. Dunbar stepped forward. "May I please see the papers?"

He waved her back to her seat. "You'll know in a minute."

Everyone leaned forward in anticipation, including Sky. What kind of information did her mother have?

Sky glanced at Cooper. His back was ramrod straight, his shoulders taut. She wanted to reach out and touch him, to let him know she would always be there for him.

The judge cleared his throat and Sky held her breath.

"I have in my hand a full pardon for Cooper Yates from the governor of Texas for all crimes he's been unjustly accused of."

A shout went up in the courtroom and everyone jumped to their feet.

The judge pounded his gavel. "Order." He turned his attention to Cooper, who was amazingly still. Sky could hardly contain her excitement. "All alleged crimes will be erased from your record. You're a free man, Mr. Yates. Right after you sign some papers for my clerk, you're free to go." He banged the gavel again. "This court is adjourned."

Cooper and Ms. Dunbar followed a clerk through a side door. He didn't look back, and that worried Sky. The crowd began to disperse.

Cait handed her some keys. "We're leaving Judd's truck for you and Cooper. We'll see you at High Five. Think big celebration."

Sky turned and ran to her mother, hugging her. "Thank you. Thank you!"

Julia drew back. "Now am I allowed in my daughter's and granddaughter's lives?"

"Yes. I'm sorry. I was desperate."

Julia kissed her cheek and Sky caught a whiff of Chanel. "Where's Kira?"

"She's at High Five."

"Richard is outside and his private jet is waiting in Austin, so I don't have a lot of time, but I want to see my baby granddaughter before I go."

"First, tell me how you got a pardon. That was beyond my wildest expectation."

Julia lifted a finely painted brow. "Do you really need to know?"

"Yes."

"I bit the bullet and flew to Huntsville to see Everett. The stupid man had my name on his visitor's list, so I was able to see him. I put a tiny tape recorder in my bra and the guard never saw or detected it. Ol' Everett was tickled out of his mind to see me, and eventually I brought the conversation around to Cooper. He said he provoked the fight by telling Cooper he would never be anything more than a cowboy, a hired hand, so what was a little prison time? And, of course, Cooper lost it."

"That bastard." Sky knew there had to be a reason. Cooper was always so gentle and compassionate.

"Mmm, and to think I married the lowlife."

"We won't discuss that."

"Good idea."

"How did you get the pardon?"

"I let Richard listen to the tape, and he said it was a shame Everett got away with that. He's attended a lot of fund-raisers here in Texas and he knows the governor, and suggested we have a talk with him. Richard's a computer geek. He pulled the tape of Cooper saving Kira from the well and showed it to him, too. And without any pressure, the governor agreed that Cooper shouldn't have to pay any longer for something that wasn't his fault."

Sky hugged her again. "Thank Richard for me."

"Oh, I will, very enthusiastically. And just so we have it on the record, you owe me big for this one."

"Anything." Sky smiled

"I want you to be happy."

"I am. Kira's mine and now Cooper's free. I'm ecstatic."

"Sugar, I'm happy about Kira. I called the ranch and

Maddie told me. Now I have to run. The man of my dreams is waiting."

"I love you." Sky got the words out before Julia could leave.

"Now, sugar, you're going to make me cry."

One more kiss and Julia sashayed away, with several men watching her.

I hope your Richard is the one. I really do.

The courtroom was empty and Sky sat down to wait for Cooper—the man of her dreams.

They were going home.

THIRTY MINUTES LATER she was still waiting. What was taking so long? Ms. Dunbar came out and looked surprised to see her.

"What are you doing here, hon?"

"I'm waiting for Cooper."

"He left a long time ago, by a side door to avoid the crowd."

Sky slowly stood. "What?"

"I thought you were waiting for him outside."

"No. Do you know where he went?"

The lawyer shook her head.

Sky grabbed her purse. "He must have gone to High Five. That's the only place he would go."

"I'm sure he has."

Sky headed for the door. "Call me after you speak to the Spencers tomorrow."

"I will."

Sky glanced back. "Thanks for everything."

"Hon, all we needed was your mother. Hell, I think I'm going to start wearing low-cut blouses and short skirts."

"Whatever works."

On the way to the truck, her cell phone rang.

"Mommy, JuJu's here and she brought me a big teddy bear." When Kira was small, she couldn't say Julia, so she'd said JuJu and it stuck.

"I know, baby, I saw her earlier."

Kira's voice dropped low. "Mommy, JuJu has a boy-friend."

"Do you like him?"

"I guess. He brought me flowers and candy."

"That was nice."

"Yeah. They're leaving. I gotta go."

"I'll be home in a few minutes."

She clicked off. Cooper wasn't there. Kira would have said so.

Where was he?

COOPER WAS IN TURMOIL and he didn't know why. He was a free man. He had his life back. So many emotions warred inside him and he couldn't identify any of them.

He'd been a loner all his life. He preferred it that way. Now people were shaking his hand, wanting to talk to him. He was the same person he'd been last week, but now he was different. Acceptable. A person to talk to.

Somehow that rubbed him the wrong way. When he needed these people, they'd shunned him. Their two-faced attitudes got to him, so he'd run.

He caught a ride with Joe Bob and walked from the gate to the barn. He needed the exercise. Staring up at that blue sky, all he could see was freedom. It was his now. But...that was the problem. He didn't know who he was supposed to be in this new freedom.

On the ride to High Five, Joe Bob had chattered away, but Cooper had a sick feeling in his gut. He'd left Sky behind. He couldn't see her, either, though. To sort through the rest of his life, he had to be alone.

And busy. That's what kept him sane.

As he reached the barn, the dogs loped to him, their tails wagging. He rubbed their heads and clutched Boots in his arms, so grateful the dog was okay.

"Did you miss me?"

They licked his hands, his face, striving to show him. They followed as he hooked a flatbed trailer to a tractor and loaded sacks of cement. He then filled a barrel with water and tossed a galvanized tub onto the trailer. The dogs jumped aboard.

The late-afternoon July sun burned his head but he was used to that. He had a job to do.

As he made his way to the well, the dogs watched him. Staring at the hole, he felt his heart pounding. Ruts showed in the dried grass, but there were no other signs of that horrid day. Except the hole. The sun had dried out the sand and it was shifting again. This time he was going to fix it for good.

He mixed water and cement and poured it into the hole. His muscles burned, but he kept working. *If he had done this the first time…* The thought tore at him. That's what was bothering him. He was responsible for the accident.

He wasn't a hero.

The pounding of hooves caught his attention. He looked up and saw Rufus ride in. The old cowboy pulled up a few feet from him.

"What are you doing, boy?"

"Making sure no one ever falls in this well again."

"Everyone's looking for you. They're worried."

"I'm fine. I just need some time."

"Don't take too long now."

Cooper sank down into the grass to wait for the cement to dry. And to wait for the pain inside him to ease.

GRAN AND THE KIDS were playing with puppets and seemed oblivious to the tension in the room. The other adults kept staring at Sky. Her nerves were frayed and any minute she was going to start screaming in frustration. This day had turned out awful, after all.

She marched into the kitchen and sat at the table, burying her face in her hands.

"Sky." Maddie touched her shoulder.

"Why is he doing this to us? Why is he hurting me like this?"

"I'm sure…"

"No." Sky jumped to her feet. "I don't want to hear your goody-two-shoes crap." She tore out the door to the veranda and plopped onto the swing.

Cait and Maddie came out and sat by her, linking their arms through hers. Her sisters' touch calmed her.

"I'm sorry. I'm about to lose it."

"Cooper needs time, that's all," Cait said. "It's been a traumatic few days."

"For me, too."

"For all of us." Maddie rubbed her arm. "Patience is not your strong suit."

"No. I'm angry and worried."

"Red-alert time?" Cait cocked an eyebrow.

"Almost. I'm starting to get really, really angry, and then I think about all he's been through and I just want to help him. But I don't know where he is."

"Cooper's a loner and he'll gravitate back to the bunk-house sooner or later." Maddie stood. "Now I have to get my brood home. Call if you need anything. I'm a few minutes away."

"I will. Thanks for calming me down." Sky took a breath. "I'll wait."

"I've got to go, too." Cait rubbed her swollen stomach. "My bundle of joy needs some rest and so do my aching feet."

Soon the house seemed so empty. Gran and Kira were playing with old hats. Sky wrapped her arms around her waist and shivered.

What if Cooper didn't come back?

He was a free man.

She shook off that thought and went back into the kitchen. Rufus came through the door, his brows knotted together in worry.

"What's wrong?" she asked.

"I found him."

"Where?"

"He's at the well and he's pouring cement down that hole. He's torturing himself."

"I'll go talk to him."

"I don't know if that's a good idea."

"Why?"

"It might be best if you let him face his own demons."

"Ru, I can't. I have to talk to him." Her voice broke on the last word.

"Do what you have to, girl."

There was only one thing she could do. A few minutes later, she saddled up and headed for the well.

CHAPTER EIGHTEEN

As she rode in she saw Cooper sitting in the grass, his hat beside him, his elbows on his knees and his hands folded between his legs. The dogs lay at his feet and a tractor and trailer were parked to the right.

The sun was sinking in the west as she dismounted. The heat of the day had eased and the landscape seemed to sigh with relief. A squirrel shimmied up a tree. Other than that there were no sounds. Just quiet. Painful quiet.

Cooper rose to his feet. "Go home, Skylar."

Skylar. They had taken so many steps backward she didn't know how to go forward. But that didn't stop her.

"What are you doing out here?" She shivered as she looked at the torn-up ground and that day came flashing back.

"Just remembering."

"There's no need for that."

"Yes. There is. I'm the reason Kira fell in that hole."

She frowned. "What are you talking about?"

"When I first found the hole after the hurricane, I dumped dirt into it and put the boards on top again. I never came back to check it and I should have."

"You were busy running a ranch. You couldn't know the sand would—"

"I should have."

"Cooper." Sky took a step toward him and he took a step back.

"It's my fault Kira is black-and-blue. It's my fault she's in more pain than any child should be."

"It's not your fault," Sky shouted, hoping to get through to him. "If it's anyone's fault, it's mine."

He glared at her.

"I'm the one who wasn't watching her. I was on the phone in the study and she was in the parlor. I know how she is and I should have been watching her closely. And if we're going to start placing blame, I guess it could be Etta's fault. She left the broom by the door. Or maybe it's Rufus's fault for checking cattle in this pasture and not noticing that Boots wasn't with him. But I'm not placing blame on anyone. I'm happy to have my daughter alive. It was an accident. That's it."

He jammed both hands through his hair, but didn't speak.

"And what if the rain hadn't caused the sand to sift? She could have been wandering out here among the cattle. She could have been trampled. Any number of things could have happened, but you saved her."

"I just keep seeing her little body..."

"Please don't blame yourself. She's better now. She and Gran are playing, and she's laughing again. You're free now. Don't—"

"Don't you see? I'm not free." He pounded his chest with his fist. "I'm still locked up inside."

"No, you're not. You opened your heart to Kira and me. Keep it open. Don't shut us out."

"I..." He looked to the north and seemed frozen in his own pain.

"And what if you hadn't dumped the dirt in? Kira would have fallen so far down that we would have never gotten her out. This would have been…her grave. None of what happened here was your fault."

He kept staring into the distance.

She swallowed back tears. "Kira's asking for you. Please come to the house and see her. That's all *I'm* asking. I know you would never intentionally hurt her, so don't do it now. Come to the house."

Sky placed her foot into the stirrup and swung into the saddle. She didn't know what else to say. It was his decision. Kneeing her horse, she galloped away, tears streaming down her cheeks.

She unsaddled Blaze and ran into the house, wiping away tears. Taking a deep breath, she walked into the parlor.

Kira was curled against Gran, who was reading to her.

"Mommy." Kira sat up and winced. "Hold me."

Sky sat down and gathered her into her arms.

"I think I'm going up to bed," Gran said. "It's been a long day. I'm so glad to have my babies home."

"We're glad, too," Kira replied.

After Gran left, Sky had to restrain herself from asking if Kira was hurting. *Don't ask.* But it was so hard. She brushed her baby's red curls from her forehead and kissed her.

Kira looked at her. "Mommy, did you see Coo?"

She swallowed hard. "Yes. He's working."

"But it's dark."

Even a four-year-old knew he couldn't work in the dark. *Don't do this, Cooper. Please come.*

But the quietness of the night met her thoughts.

"How about some ice cream?"

"No." Kira settled against her. "I already had some with Etta's cake."

Total despair washed over Sky and she didn't have the strength to keep fighting. But how did she stop?

Kira raised her head just then and a smile split her face. "Coo!" she shouted, slipping off Sky's lap and limping to the man standing in the doorway.

"Coo. Coo."

Cooper hurried to her and lifted her gently into his arms. "Hey, sunshine."

Kira wrapped her arms around his neck. "I knew you'd come."

Cooper sat on the sofa and held her. Sky didn't say a word. She was just so happy he was here.

Kira slowly drifted to sleep against his chest. Sky saw him looking at the blue spots on Kira's legs, her ankles, her arms and face. How long would he keep blaming himself?

She got to her feet. "Would you like to carry her to bed?"

Without a word, he followed Sky up the stairs and into the room. He gently laid Kira in bed and covered her with a sheet. Kissing her cheek, he said, "Sweet dreams, sunshine."

He turned and his eyes met Sky's. She saw all the torment revealed there and she had to do something.

"I love you. Kira loves you. Why isn't that enough?"

"You don't understand." His voice was hoarse.

"Explain it to me, please."

"I've always been the outcast, the outlaw, and I'm comfortable in that skin. I knew my boundaries. But now everyone wants to shake my hand, pat me on the back, and I don't know how to deal with that. I'm still the same person, but suddenly I'm not."

Now she understood. He was struggling to find himself. Blaming himself for the accident was a way to keep the old Cooper alive. Everyone would hate him, and he'd learned to deal with that kind of treatment.

"You're the same to me. That's all that matters."

"No, it isn't. Everett once told me that I was a hired hand, a cowboy, and that's all I would ever be. He was right. You and Kira deserve more than that."

"Cooper..."

He held up a hand to stop her as she moved forward. "Todd Spencer is the type of man you're attracted to, suave, educated and with money."

"Oh, please, don't even compare yourself to that unfeeling bastard."

"But you loved him."

"I thought I loved him, but he showed his true colors quickly. I'm a different person now. And so are you."

"But I have nothing to offer you. I'm still the hired hand."

"Cooper." This time she moved close to him and wrapped her arms around his waist. He didn't hug her back. Searching for the magic to put them back together, she placed her hand flat against his chest. His heart pounded against her palm. "This is all I want. Your heart. Your love."

"Red," he groaned, and cupped her face. He stared into her eyes for a moment and then his lips covered hers. All the emotions he was trying to deny burst forth in his kiss, and his touch. She felt the cuts on his hands and the fire in him. Then heat and need took over and they renewed that special connection they shared. But only for a minute. He pulled away and was out the door before she could stop him.

She started to go after him, but halted. He had to find his way back to her himself. And he had to learn to accept the new emotions in him—to accept the free Cooper Yates. She couldn't force it.

Maddie was right when she'd said that Sky wasn't patient, but now she would learn to be. She'd wait forever.

For Cooper.

THE NEXT FEW DAYS WERE difficult, but Sky got through them. Her bright spot was Kira, who was getting better every day. The bruises were fading, as was the limp. Her baby was growing strong again.

Ms. Dunbar sealed the deal with the Spencers by agreeing to a onetime settlement. Her daughter's education and medical bills would be taken care of for the rest of her life. The amount was staggering, but Sky accepted it for Kira. Ms. Dunbar even managed to wrangle her own fee from the Spencers.

Every morning Kira rushed downstairs to have breakfast with Coop, and in the evenings she stood at the kitchen door waiting for him. It didn't matter if he was late, just as long as he came.

Sky knew in her heart that their love would win him over. She just had to be patient, but she was really beginning to hate that word. The old Skylar would go on full red alert and confront him, demanding that he love her.

The grown-up Skylar would give him time.

COOPER WAS BUSY harvesting the corn and he tried not to think about Red, but found that impossible. She was everywhere because she was in his heart.

He dismounted at Crooked Creek and sat beneath an

old cypress, watching the shadows of the branches sway in the water.

He was so tired of thinking. He finally had to admit he wasn't at fault for the accident. Red didn't blame him, and that got him through and made him see things clearer. Still, the emotions warred inside him.

His thoughts always brought him back to the same problem: he had nothing to offer Red. He wanted to give her the world, but all he'd given her was pain. God, why couldn't he just be normal and not care? Just take everything she was offering.

Pride.

His damn pride!

When he was at his lowest, his pride was all he had. He couldn't sacrifice that. It would make him less of a man. And sometimes a man had to be exactly who he was, pride and all.

He heard movement and saw Rufus dismount. "What are you doing out here, boy?"

"Taking a breather and thinking."

Ru sank down by him. "You gonna think yourself to death."

"Yeah." He picked up a rock and skipped it across the water. "What's freedom, Ru, if you can't have the woman you want?"

"It ain't nothing."

"Yeah." He skipped another rock.

"I'm no rocket scientist, but it seems to me if you want your freedom and Sky, then you make it happen. Decide what you want and do it. This brooding ain't good."

"Mmm."

A comfortable silence passed as they watched the shadows on the water.

"They'll be through harvesting tomorrow," Ru said. "That place in Giddings will have the corn ground into feed in a couple of days, so I guess we better get started on a shed to put the bags in to keep 'em out of the weather."

"Yep. We better get started."

Ru rose to his feet. "I'll check and see if Nell has some two-by-fours and tin."

As the August sun bore down and scorched the landscape, Cooper sucked in a long, heated breath. This was where he started to change his life and accept everything that had been given back to him. "No. I'll do it."

Ru glanced back, his eyebrows drawn together. "You'll do it?"

"Yep. I'm reclaiming my life."

Thirty minutes later he walked into Walker's General Store with pride and with confidence.

"Good afternoon, Cooper," Nell said, as if she was an old friend and not the woman who'd refused to sell anything to him for years.

"Hey, Cooper, what do ya need?" Luther called from the back.

"Two-by-fours, tin and lead-headed nails."

"Pull your truck around back and I'll load it for ya."

"Thanks." He tipped his hat to Nell and paused at the door as Charlie, the vet, came through it.

"Good to see you, Cooper." Charlie shook his hand as if it were a pump handle. "You know, when I was at High Five, I saw that heifer in the corral walking around as big as day."

"She's going to make it. I'm letting her get stronger before introducing her back into the herd."

"Good idea." Charlie nodded. "Give her about six months."

"I will." Cooper stepped outside. "I have to go. Luther's gonna load my truck."

"Sure. If you need any vet services, you just call, you hear? I'll give you a discount."

"Thanks. I appreciate that."

As he walked away, Coop smiled for the first time in days. This wasn't hard at all. He could do it. Freedom was exactly what you made it, and he was going to embrace his. It was what he wanted. He knew that now. And he knew what else he wanted.

He just had to make it happen.

SKY OPENED THE BOOKS for a Belle sisters business meeting and had her siblings' full attention. The kids were in the parlor watching a movie with Gran, and Val was asleep.

"I'm happy to say High Five is in the black this month, and Mr. Bardwell has started hauling sand and gravel again. That's extra money in our coffers."

"That's wonderful," Maddie said. "How are things with you and Cooper?"

"He's back to ignoring me. I thought freedom would mean the world to him, but he's still locked up within himself."

"Give him time," Maddie suggested, her expression sad.

"I am."

"You are?" Cait raised a skeptical eyebrow.

"Yes." Sky gritted her teeth, daring her older sister to say one more thing, which she did.

"We need to write this down somewhere, because it's probably never going to happen again."

She stuck out her tongue and then laughed. And, oh, it felt good to release some of the tension inside her.

Sky closed the books and scooted her chair forward. "We have to decide what to do about High Five. We keep putting it off."

"I know." Cait stroked her protruding stomach. "It's hard to let go of a legacy."

"I think it's more letting go of Dad that's so hard." Maddie brushed back her blond hair with a wistful gaze.

"But he's always in our hearts," Sky said, feeling her throat close up. "Besides, I'll be here to run things until we decide."

"Good." Maddie smiled. "I'd hate for you to move Kira. She's doing so well and it would break Georgie's heart, not to mention mine. And Gran's. And everyone else's in the family."

"I'm not leaving. I have my kid and I don't have to run anymore. And there's a stubborn cowboy I haven't broken yet."

"Oh, this sounds interesting." Cait lifted an eyebrow.

"Enough about me." Sky waved a hand at her sisters. "What's going on in your lives? I haven't talked to either of you in a couple of days."

Maddie brightened. "My adoption of the kids became final. I'm legally their mother."

"Congratulations," Sky and Cait echoed.

"Thank you. We had a big celebration." Suddenly Maddie's expression changed. "This weekend we're meeting Trisha and her husband in San Antonio, so she can visit with the kids. She hasn't seen Val since she was born."

"That's kind of like poking yourself in the eye kind of fun," Sky said.

"She is their biological mother." Maddie shifted in her seat. "She canceled the first arranged meeting. They were going on some kind of trip or something. I just wish the kids were more enthusiastic about seeing her."

"Why, for heaven's sake?" Cait asked. "I wouldn't want to see anyone who hit me, either."

"It's just difficult, and I want to make it as easy as possible on my kids."

"You will," Sky assured her. "Nobody does gooder-than-good with a smile better than you."

"It's not that easy with Trisha, but Walker and I are planning to do some fun stuff, like SeaWorld, with the kids—family time to make the visit not such a big thing."

"Smart idea." Sky glanced at Cait. "What's up with you? You're very quiet."

Cait rubbed her stomach. "We found out the sex of the baby this morning and I'm a little in shock."

"Why?"

Cait held up two fingers.

"What the hell does that mean?" Sky asked.

"Not one but two babies."

"Oh, my." Maddie jumped up and hugged Cait. "A girl and a boy?"

"No. Two boys."

"How exciting!" Sky ran over and embraced her sister.

"Wouldn't you know Judd would be shooting double."

They burst out laughing.

A knock at the door interrupted them.

"That's probably my not-so-patient daughter." Sky opened the door and Cooper stood there. Her heart hammered against her ribs.

"Coop…"

"May I speak to y'all?"

Y'all? Why did he want to speak to all of them?

"Sure, cowboy, come on in," Cait said. "I'd get up but these days it's harder and harder to do that."

"That's okay. This won't take long." He removed his hat and placed it on the desk. For the first time, Sky noticed he held a manila folder in his hand. And he was freshly shaved and his jeans and shirt were clean, as if this was a special occasion.

"Ever since I can remember I've wanted to have my own ranch, but I got sidetracked by a lot of bad luck. Now I'm a free man and I still have that dream."

What? Was he leaving? *No, no, no!* She would not let him. But how could she stop him?

He opened the folder. "I've done a lot of research and I've checked at the Giddings courthouse on land that has been sold recently in this area." He drew out a piece of paper. "I have the down payment and I think I'm offering a fair price. I'm hoping you'll consider selling High Five."

Total silence followed those words.

"May I see that, please?" Cait asked, all business.

He handed her the paper. "I know it's not for sale, but I wish you'd think about it. High Five is my home now and I'd like to stay here."

Cait perused the paper. "Cowboy, where'd you get money like this?"

"I've socked away almost every dime from my wages. It adds up when you don't spend it."

"Could you give us a few minutes?"

"Sure." He picked up his hat and walked out.

Sky jerked the paper out of Cait's hand. A twenty-year note. Payments. He had it all worked out. He was serious. Suddenly everything became clear. His pride.

He wanted something of his own—to offer her. God, she hoped she had that right.

"Did you know about this?" Cait asked.

"No."

"We were just talking about High Five and its future." Maddie took the paper. "Now we have to decide. Personally, my life is with Walker, and he has land in back of our house and in High Cotton. I can't see myself ever coming back here to work."

Cait rose with effort. "My life is with Judd on the Southern Cross." She looked at Sky. "What do you think?"

Sky swallowed. "I think Dad would want High Five to continue to prosper, and it has been prospering because of Cooper. I say yes." She frowned. "Do you think he'll kick me out?"

"Oh, please." Cait grabbed the paper back. "We all know this is about Cooper's pride. I swear he's as stubborn as a Belle." She sat at the desk. "Let's see. This is entirely too high. Any objections?"

"No," Sky and Maddie chorused.

Cait reached for a pen and a calculator. "Coop worked fourteen- and sixteen-hour days and only got paid for eight. We need to adjust the figures. And do we really need a down payment?"

"I don't," Maddie said.

Sky shook her head. She just wanted Cooper.

"Okay." Cait handed them another paper. "Look at that and see if you agree, especially to the conditions I've added."

"Agreed," Maddie said.

Sky glanced over her shoulder. "For once, big sister, I'm glad you're so bossy."

"Then we're all in agreement?"

They nodded their heads and Maddie called Cooper back in.

"Here's the deal, cowboy." Cait handed him the paper. His eyes narrowed. "That's..."

"That's the way it's going to be—if you want to own High Five. The animals and equipment come with the sale. All mineral rights remain with the sisters. You have the surface rights. We don't require a down payment and Gran stays on the property in this house until her death. Etta and Rufus will continue to stay also. We're selling you two-thirds. Sky retains her third. Any questions?"

"I guess not."

Cait reached out and touched his hand. "You're the only person I'd entrust the ranch to. You've more than earned it."

"Thank you. I won't let you down. High Five will continue to move forward."

"I have no doubt." She pushed herself to her feet. "I'll have the family lawyer draw up the papers. There'll be two new deeds, one for Sky and one for you." Cait paused, her hand on her stomach. "Or he could just draw up one deed with both your names on it. What do you say, cowboy?"

Cooper raised his head and met Sky's eyes "What do you think, Red?"

"Could we have a moment alone, please?"

Her sisters quietly left, closing the door.

She placed her hands on her hips. "What does one deed mean to you?"

"It means you and I will run this ranch together—as husband and wife."

All the emotions, all the patience she'd been holding inside suddenly snapped, and white anger suffused her body. She went into full red-alert mode and words started flying out of her mouth. "And you think I'll marry you after the pain you put me through? You think I'll forget so easily that you let your stubborn male ego get in the way of us? I don't need you to own a ranch. I don't need you to be free. I just need *you,* and if you think—"

"I love you."

"W-what?" She spit and sputtered and ran out of steam.

His eyes held hers. "You understand me better than anyone, Red."

"I…" Forgiveness came just that easily because she did understand him and his torment. She flew across the room and into his arms. He caught her in a bearlike hug.

"I'm sorry this was so difficult for me," he mumbled into her hair. "I'm sorry I hurt you." He kissed her neck, her cheek, the corner of her lips, and covered her mouth with aching sweetness that turned into a roaring flame.

She ran her fingers through his hair, knocking his hat to the floor. He held her tightly, running his hand up her back as the kiss went on and on into an eternity that wasn't long enough.

Coming up for air, she rested her face against his. "I love you. Please don't ever do that to me again."

"I won't." He kissed her forehead.

Kissing his cheek, she said, "Please don't blame yourself for what happened to Kira."

He took a long breath. "I'm not. I actually heard what you were trying to tell me. I guess I was still trying to be the bad guy, the outlaw."

She looped her arms around his neck. "You will always be my outlaw."

Coop drew back and looked into her eyes again. "I...I love you more than life itself. Will you marry me? Stubborn pride and all?"

"You're in luck. I love stubborn cowboys." Sky played with a button on his shirt. "What would you have done if Cait and Maddie had said no?"

"Then I would have been *your* hired hand for the rest of my life."

"I hate to tell you this, cowboy, but you still will be."

He laughed and she loved that robust sound. It was beautiful, freeing and uplifting. His eyes were clear. The pain was gone, and finally he was truly free.

"I have big plans for High Five. With you by my side, we can make it happen."

Sky leaned her head back and he took his time trailing fiery kisses up her throat to her chin. "I think I'll spend more time with my daughter, and I might cook something."

"Lord help us."

She poked him in the ribs. "And...we might start thinking about a brother or sister for Kira."

"Whoa, Red, I'm just starting to accept my new life."

She undid a button on his shirt. "My mother would appreciate a thank-you."

"I'll call her first thing." He sucked in a breath as Sky undid more buttons. "When she walked into that courtroom all flamboyant and daring, it brought back my years at the Rocking C. I guess I shut down completely."

"Yes, you did." Sky pulled his shirt out of his jeans. "And you're lucky I'm so forgiving."

"We need to let Cait and Maddie know our decision."

"I think they already know." She kissed his chest and he sucked in a breath.

"Red," he breathed raggedly. "I don't want you to stop, but anyone could walk in."

She took a step backward and locked the door. Unbuttoning her blouse, she said, "Oh, cowboy, haven't you heard I'm the wild sister?"

EPILOGUE

Two months later…

"KIRA, DO YOU HAVE Mommy's shoes?"

Sky ran around the bedroom in a long white slip, her hair up in curls. It was her wedding day and her nerves were getting the best of her.

"Your dress is beautiful," Maddie said, staring at the white silk-and-lace creation Sky's mother had mailed from Paris.

Julia couldn't make the wedding. She and Richard already had a trip planned. Sky wasn't upset. Her mother had been there when she'd needed her the most. That's what counted.

Cait fingered the dress on the bed. "It's gorgeous, but I don't know if it's right for a sister who said she'd never get married and never be forced into all the hoopla of a wedding."

"Shut up, Cait. No, I didn't mean that."

"Come on, bitchy, if you turn one hundred and eighty degrees on me, I'll flip out. And you don't want to do that to a pregnant woman."

Maddie guided Sky to a stool in front of the mirrored dresser. "Why are you so nervous?"

"Because I'm happy." Unable to stop it, she felt a tear slip from her eye.

"Then relax and enjoy this day." Cait pushed herself to her feet.

Kira appeared in the doorway in nothing but her panties. She ran to the bed and fished out Sky's shoes from beneath it. All the dark bruises were gone and her knee wasn't swollen. Happiness had made a big difference in Kira. And in Sky.

Her daughter handed her the shoes. "I was playing with them. Now I gotta go. Gran and me are getting dressed. Wait till you see us." In a flash she was gone.

Sky grimaced. "I hope that's good."

"Don't worry," Maddie said. "Our Gran is back and they'll be beautiful. Besides, you already know what Kira's dress looks like. So what could happen?"

"I'm worried what she'll put on her head."

Her sisters laughed and then Maddie asked, "How is Kira liking her new room?"

"So far so good. She's excited she has her own room, like Haley and Georgie. And Cooper hooked up monitors in her room and ours. We can hear every sound she makes."

"So Coop moves in tonight?"

"He's already moved his things," she told Cait. "Tonight will be the first night he sleeps in his own house." The sale had gone through yesterday and High Five now had new owners—Cooper and Skylar Belle Yates.

Maddie picked up the gown. "Time to get you dressed."

"The youngest Belle sister is getting married." Cait helped Maddie to remove the plastic cover. "I can't help but think that Dad would be proud of our husbands."

"Yeah." Sky turned on the stool, her voice nostalgic. "I wish he was here to walk me down the aisle."

They were silent as their hearts filled with sadness for a father they loved.

"Don't do this to a pregnant woman." Cait wiped away a tear. "We have Gran and that's the next best thing."

"Yeah," they shouted in unison, and gave each other a high five as the door opened. Gran and Kira stood there.

Kira looked like an angel in her white dress and Mary Jane shoes. On her head was perched a floppy white hat with white ribbons trailing down the back. In her hand she held a basket of colored rose petals. Everything was perfect.

Gran wore a lavender suit and a lavender wide-brim hat.

"We look—" Kira glanced up at her great-grandmother. "What do we look like?"

"Texas Belles," Gran replied.

"Yeah, we're Texas Belles." Kira nodded, the hat bobbing.

Sky clapped her hands. "You're beautiful."

"Now can we get married?"

"Oh yes, let's go get married."

"To Coo, Mommy?"

"Yes, to Coo."

The ceremony was in the parlor, just as her sisters' had been, and it was the happiest day of Sky's life. When she saw Cooper in a dark suit and white shirt, her breath lodged in her throat. He was so handsome and he seemed almost a stranger—until he grinned. Then she knew he was her outlaw.

The ceremony was short and special, with family and friends present. She took her vows with her sisters on her left side, and Kira wedged between them so she didn't miss a thing.

When Cooper slipped rings onto her finger, she gasped. They were her grandmother's rings. She glanced at Cooper and then at Gran, in the front row, who winked. Now Sky understood why Gran had given her Grandfather Bart's wedding band for Cooper. She and Cooper would carry on the legacy of High Five.

Rufus and Chance had been barbecuing since early morning. The whole town was invited to the reception at High Five, and they spilled out onto the lawn and the veranda. Etta kept bring more potato salad and beans to the serving table. Everyone visited and enjoyed the first barbecue at High Five in a long time.

Solomon interrupted the party, but Cooper and the kids took him back to his pen.

Cooper talked to his neighbors without a problem. He had faced all his demons and won. The victory was his.

Sky sat on the front stoop and waited for her husband, who was talking to a couple of ranchers. Cait and Judd cuddled together in the porch swing. On the bottom step, Walker had his arm around Maddie's waist, and she was resting her head on his shoulder. Gran relaxed in a rocker behind them, holding a sleeping Val.

Happiness was all around Sky. And family.

Cooper strolled over and sank down beside her. He kissed her lips. "I haven't had a minute alone with you."

She pushed his hair from his forehead. "We will later."

"I'm living for that." He grinned.

She twisted the rings on her finger. "I can't believe your pride let you take these rings."

"Miss Dorie—"

"Gran," she corrected.

"Gran wouldn't let me refuse. She said you had

Grandfather Bart's for me and the owners of High Five had to have the matching rings."

"I love them." Sky glanced down at her hand. "I've wanted them since I was a little girl."

He put his arm around her. "A dream come true."

She kissed his cheek, loving his woodsy scent. "You're my dream."

They kissed deeply and then watched Kira and Georgie sitting on an ice chest, blowing bubbles from bottles that Maddie had bought for them. Haley sat at their feet, bouncing the bubbles back to them. Bursts of giggles ensued.

"I've been watching her to make sure she doesn't run a lot," Cooper said.

"Me, too." Sky sighed. "It feels so good to share the responsibility."

"I'm here forever, Red. I hate that it takes so long for the adoption papers to go through."

"You're already her father so it doesn't matter."

"I suppose." He stroked her arm. "Aren't you going to open the letter?"

Her father's attorney had given her a letter, as she knew he would on her wedding day. Cait and Maddie had gotten one and she knew these were his last words to her, his youngest daughter, the wild child.

She slipped a finger under the flap and pulled out a single sheet of paper. The light was fading, but she could still read the words: "Enjoy the rewards of growing up, my spitfire! Love, Dad. P.S. Take care of my grandbaby."

She would.

A sob blocked Sky's throat. Kira crawled onto Cooper's lap and he pulled both of them close. Sky had

the man she loved, her child, her sisters, her grandmother and extended family.

She was finally home.

And so was Cooper.

*****

*Fan favorite Leslie Kelly is bringing her readers
a fantasy so scandalous,
we're calling it FORBIDDEN!*

*Look for
PLAY WITH ME
Available February 2010 from Harlequin® Blaze™.*

"AREN'T YOU GOING TO SAY 'Fly me' or at least 'Welcome aboard'?"

Amanda Bauer didn't. The softly muttered word that actually came out of her mouth was a lot less welcoming. And had fewer letters. Four, to be exact.

The man shook his head and tsked. "Not exactly the friendly skies. Haven't caught the spirit yet this morning?"

"Make one more airline-slogan crack and you'll be walking to Chicago," she said.

He nodded once, then pushed his sunglasses onto the top of his tousled hair. The move revealed blue eyes that matched the sky above. And yeah. They were twinkling. Damn it.

"Understood. Just, uh, promise me you'll say 'Coffee, tea or me' at least once, okay? Please?"

Amanda tried to glare, but that twinkle sucked the annoyance right out of her. She could only draw in a slow breath as he climbed into the plane. As she watched her passenger disappear into the small jet, she had to wonder about the trip she was about to take.

Coffee and tea they had, and he was welcome to them. But her? Well, she'd never even considered making a move on a customer before. Talk about unprofessional.

And yet...

Something inside her suddenly wanted to take a chance, to be a little outrageous.

How long since she had done indecent things—or decent ones, for that matter—with a sexy man? Not since before they'd thrown all their energies into expanding Clear-Blue Air, at the very least. She hadn't had time for a lunch date, much less the kind of lust-fest she'd enjoyed in her younger years. The kind that lasted for entire weekends and involved not leaving a bed except to grab the kind of sensuous food that could be smeared onto—and eaten off—someone else's hot, naked, sweat-tinged body.

She closed her eyes, her hand clenching tight on the railing. Her heart fluttered in her chest and she tried to make herself move. But she couldn't—not climbing up, but not backing away, either. Not physically, and not in her head.

Was she really considering this? God, she hadn't even looked at the stranger's left hand to make sure he was available. She had no idea if he was actually attracted to her or just an irrepressible flirt. Yet something inside was telling her to take a shot with this man.

It was crazy. Something she'd never considered. Yet right now, at this moment, she was definitely considering it. If he was available...could she do it? Seduce a stranger. Have an anonymous fling, like something out of a blue movie on late-night cable?

She didn't know. All she knew was that the flight to Chicago was a short one so she had to decide quickly. And as she put her foot on the bottom step and began to climb up, Amanda suddenly had to wonder if she was about to embark on the ride of her life.

Sold, bought, bargained for or bartered

He'll take his...

Bride on Approval

Whether there's a debt to be paid,
a will to be obeyed or a business
to be saved...she has no choice
but to say, "I do"!

PURE PRINCESS,
BARTERED BRIDE
by *Caitlin Crews*
#2894

Available February 2010!

LARGER-PRINT BOOKS!
GET 2 FREE LARGER-PRINT NOVELS PLUS
2 FREE GIFTS!

HARLEQUIN

Super Romance

Exciting, emotional, unexpected!

YES! Please send me 2 FREE LARGER-PRINT Harlequin® Superromance® novels and my 2 FREE gifts (gifts are worth about $10). After receiving them, if I don't wish to receive any more books, I can return the shipping statement marked "cancel." If I don't cancel, I will receive 6 brand-new novels every month and be billed just $5.44 per book in the U.S. or $5.99 per book in Canada. That's a saving of over 15% off the cover price! It's quite a bargain! Shipping and handling is just 50¢ per book in the U.S. and 75¢ per book in Canada.* I understand that accepting the 2 free books and gifts places me under no obligation to buy anything. I can always return a shipment and cancel at any time. Even if I never buy another book from Harlequin, the two free books and gifts are mine to keep forever.

139 HDN E4JY 339 HDN E4KC

Name _____ (PLEASE PRINT) _____

Address _____ Apt. # _____

City _____ State/Prov. _____ Zip/Postal Code _____

Signature (if under 18, a parent or guardian must sign) _____

Mail to the **Harlequin Reader Service:**
IN U.S.A.: P.O. Box 1867, Buffalo, NY 14240-1867
IN CANADA: P.O. Box 609, Fort Erie, Ontario L2A 5X3

Not valid for current subscribers to Harlequin Superromance Larger-Print books.

**Are you a current subscriber to Harlequin Superromance books
and want to receive the larger-print edition?
Call 1-800-873-8635 today!**

* Terms and prices subject to change without notice. Prices do not include applicable taxes. N.Y. residents add applicable sales tax. Canadian residents will be charged applicable provincial taxes and GST. Offer not valid in Quebec. This offer is limited to one order per household. All orders subject to approval. Credit or debit balances in a customer's account(s) may be offset by any other outstanding balance owed by or to the customer. Please allow 4 to 6 weeks for delivery. Offer available while quantities last.

Your Privacy: Harlequin Books is committed to protecting your privacy. Our Privacy Policy is available online at www.eHarlequin.com or upon request from the Reader Service. From time to time we make our lists of customers available to reputable third parties who may have a product or service of interest to you. If you would prefer we not share your name and address, please check here. ☐

Help us get it right—We strive for accurate, respectful and relevant communications. To clarify or modify your communication preferences, visit us at www.ReaderService.com/consumerschoice.

HSRLP10

HARLEQUIN® *Blaze*™

*It all started
with a few naughty books....*

As a member of the Red Tote Book Club,
Carol Snow has been studying works of
classic erotic literature…but Carol doesn't
believe in love…or marriage. It's going to take
another kind of classic—Charles Dickens's
A Christmas Carol—and a little otherworldly
persuasion to convince her to go after her
own sexily ever after.

Cuddle up with

Her Sexy Valentine

by STEPHANIE BOND

Available February 2010

---

red-hot reads

PREGNANT BRIDES

*Inexperienced and expecting,
they're forced to marry!*

Bestselling Harlequin Presents author ·

Lynne Graham

brings you the second story
in this exciting new trilogy:

RUTHLESS MAGNATE, CONVENIENT WIFE
#2892
Available February 2010

Also look for

GREEK TYCOON, INEXPERIENCED MISTRESS
#2900
Available March 2010

HP12892

Whirlwind Secrets
DEBRA COWAN

HE *WILL* UNCOVER
THE TRUTH!

Russ Baldwin has learned from harsh experience
to look twice at people. When his business partner,
Miss Lydia Kent, moves into town, he goes
on high alert....

Russ's watchful eyes rattle Lydia. She must keep
her noble, yet underground, activities—and
her emotions—tightly under wraps. When Russ
realizes his curvy, sweet-talkin' co-owner has
hidden depths, he's determined to uncover them!

*Available February
wherever you buy books.*